Abduction of

Life

Nanci M. Pattenden

Detective Hodgins Victorian Murder Mysteries

Body in the Harbour

Death on Duchess Street

Corpses for Christmas

Books 1 to 3 Collection

Homicide on the Homestead

United in Holy Deadlock

Generation Witch

Rebirth

D.E.M.ON. Tales Series

Assassin Eco-Corpses

Bobcat Got Your Tongue?

A Craptacular Understatement

Double Dog Dare Ya

Even Equines Don't Like Liver

Frozen Foes & Dominos

Growing Up Grim

Hoodoo In The Loo

ACKNOWLEDGMENTS

I'd like to say a great big thanks to Omar and Ashley, owners of Cardinal Press Espresso Bar in Newmarket for providing a wonderful environment in which to work. The coffee is constantly flowing and the treats are always yummy.

As always, thanks to my editor, MJ, of Infinite Pathways, and Chris, my graphics guru.

THANK YOU

CHAPTER ONE

Detective Albert Hodgins sat behind his desk at Station House Four, flipping through the reports. Routine stuff. Nothing for a detective to get involved with. All in all, the start of a long, boring day. The constables had been busy with thefts, missing husbands who turned up drunk somewhere, and run-of-the-mill arguments. A quick read-through of the reports and a signature was all that was required of Hodgins.

Constable Henry Barnes knocked on the door to the detective's office and entered with another report to be initialled. His lopsided grin let the detective know it wasn't a serious offence. "You might get a chuckle out of this, sir." He placed the report on the desk, turning the paper so Hodgins could read it.

The detective snickered as he read. "Don't imagine that poor bugger thought it terribly funny. Still a might chilly in the mornings to be running around in his underthings." He kept reading and stopped laughing.

"Councilman Smith? I wonder if that skinner knew who she was luring into the alley? Didn't catch her?"

Barnes shook his head. "No, but from the description, I think it's Nell. Only thief I know of with a limp and huge wart over her left eye."

Hodgins initialled the page and slid it back to Barnes. "That description paints a truly ugly picture, but Nell is quite a looker, despite the wart. Hate to say it, but she'd make a much better living off her body."

The constable picked up the report. "Yes, she'd make good money as a dollybird, but the city has too many already. Too bad she hasn't taken to any of those jobs you lined up for her."

"You forgot the nanny job. She seemed content with the children. It was a jealous wife that ended that one, if I recall. Maybe when you and Violet start a family?"

Barnes shook his head. "Violet is not that understanding."

The front door slammed, halting their conversation. Someone ran through the station, stopping at the detective's door.

"Harrington. Has something happened?" Hodgins pushed his chair away from the desk.

"Sir." He leaned against the door frame, taking a few deep breaths, stooping from his unusual height to avoid banging his head. "Woman's been found, dead. Doc thinks it might be suicide, but isn't positive. Asked for you to come 'round."

Hodgins stood. "Barnes, see if you can find Nell then see if Smith wants her charged. He may prefer to keep it quiet." He put on his overcoat and followed Constable Harrington through the station.

"It's at 32 John Street, sir. Mrs. Holiwell's ladies boarding house. I've got a cab waiting."

The horse made good time, as the streets weren't too busy. Hodgins paid the driver and told him not to wait. Doctor Stonehouse's buggy sat at the curb, horse dozing. He straightened the blanket on the mare's back, then followed Harrington inside.

A woman stood outside one of the rooms, wringing her hands. Hodgins couldn't tell if she was upset or angry.

Harrington gestured towards the woman. "Detective Hodgins, this is Mrs. Holiwell. She runs the place."

"How could she have done such a thing? I run a respectable house. If word gets around my boarders are lunatics that kill themselves, no one will want to stay here. She seemed so… normal." Holiwell peeked into the room, wincing at the sight of the young woman laying on the bed.

Hodgins looked into the small room. "Nothing seems amiss. No signs of a struggle."

The doctor closed up his bag and turned his head towards the detective's voice. "Medicine bottle by her bed. Could be she died from her illness, although I've been told she didn't have anything serious. Might be she took too much medicine at once. I'll know more after the autopsy. May I take the body now?"

"Give me a few minutes, doctor." Hodgins turned to the landlady. "I'll need to ask you a few questions about the young woman as soon as I have a look through her room."

It took less than five minutes to go through the deceased's lodgings. She had three dresses in the wardrobe, stockings and underclothes in the drawers of a bureau, and one letter, unopened, on the desk. The doctor had already taken the medicine bottle and placed it in his bag. A coat tree stood near the door. A pair of high-top lady's boots sat under a woolen winter coat; a lighter spring cape hung beside it. Hodgins stepped into the hall.

"She's all yours, Doctor. Harrington can lend a hand getting her downstairs." Hodgins turned to Mrs. Holiwell. "Is there someplace where we can talk in private?"

"Sitting room'll be empty. All my ladies are at work."

He followed her downstairs, taking in the surroundings. Not a speck of dust on the banister. The steps, hallway, and front entrance swept clean. Some of the boarding houses he'd been called to were seedy and filthy, full of rats and other vermin. He suspected the ladies that boarded here were shop clerks or employed in an office.

Mrs. Holiwell led him into a room at the front of the house. The furniture looked old, but kept in good repair. A low fire burned in the fireplace as a slight overnight chill lingered. The fireplace mantle held cheap statues of horses and two candlesticks, candles burnt part-way down. Several paintings hung on the wall of the sitting room. One of King William IV, along with garden scenes and more horses. She sat in a high-back chair near the hearth and gestured for the detective to sit. "What is it you need to know?"

"Straight to the point. I like that." He took his notebook out of his pocket. "There was a letter on her desk, addressed to Miss Annabel Jackson. Can I assume that is the woman who rented the room?"

She nodded.

"Do you know if she had family? A beau? Who visited her?"

"She mentioned a brother, Samuel, I believe. She occasionally had gentlemen callers. They were always polite and well dressed. Didn't mind chatting while they waited for her. Always brought her back well before curfew. Two, maybe three different beaus courted her. I don't believe there was anything serious yet. Don't know their names.

Why would she top herself? Can't believe she'd do such a thing."

Hodgins made notes as she spoke. "You think she killed herself?"

She shrugged. "Only had a simple ailment. Nothing that would kill her."

"Interesting. These gentlemen callers, are you certain you don't know their names? She never addressed them? Maybe one of your other residents could provide more information on them?"

"She was close to Gertie Dickson. Has the room across the hall from her. They both work at Elliot and Company, druggist, as clerks. Over at Yonge and Front."

"Yes, I know the place. The medicine bottle in her room, do you know what it was for?"

"She complained of stomach problems two days ago. Gertie fetched a doctor, and he prescribed the medicine."

"Do you know his name? Is he a doctor you use regularly?"

"No. Gertie said someone recommended him. Cousin, I believe. Sailor. Hmm. Let me think. Had a peculiar name. Should be able to recall." She tapped her fingers on the arms of the chair as she thought. Mrs. Holiwell stopped and snapped her fingers. "Doctor Coward. Imagine. A doctor with such a strange name."

Hodgins wrote the name, then twirled his pencil. "I've come across that last name before. William Coward. A seventeenth century English writer. Most of his works were considered blasphemous and burned. Coincidently, he was also a physician." *Wonder if they're related?* "Anyway, can you think of any reason she'd have for killing herself?"

"No. Not at all. Other than being ill, she seemed quite happy."

Hodgins stood. "I think that's all for now, Mrs. Holiwell. I'll just get the letter from her desk. If you could lock up the room until the doctor's finding are in, just in case? I'll inform her family and employer."

Once Hodgins retrieved the letter, he found Harrington waiting on the front step, the doctor's carriage gone.

"Shall I hail a hansom cab, sir?"

"Not yet. We need to pay a visit to Miss Jackson's employer and inform him of her death. I'd also like to speak with Miss Dickson, who also worked at the same business. She's another boarder here, as well as Miss Jackson's friend and co-worker. We can walk. It's just over at Yonge and Front. Should only take a quarter hour to get there."

The spring air was fresh, and not overly chilly. The walk along Front Street in the heat of summer wasn't pleasant as the high temperatures increased the stench from the waterfront. Fortunately, today the wind blew south, keeping the smell bearable in the temperate weather.

When they arrived, only one woman was visible in the pharmacy. She appeared to be in her twenties, the same age as the deceased. Hodgins waved away the gentlemen who approached and went straight to the lone lady.

"Excuse me. Are you Miss Dickson?"

"Yes. How may I assist you?" She looked up at the constable, then back at the detective.

"Is there someplace we can talk? I also need to speak with your employer."

"Certainly. This way."

She led them to the back offices, stopping at a desk outside a closed door. "Good morning, Mr. Stokes. These officers would like to speak with Mr. Elliot."

Stokes raised an eyebrow and stood. "I'll see if he's available." He knocked on the door, then entered, closing it behind him. A minute later, he returned. "Mr. Elliot will see you now."

Hodgins gestured for Miss Dickson to enter, then followed her in. Harrington stayed with Mr. Stokes, filling him in, as per Hodgins' instructions on the way over. The detective knew people would sometimes tell a constable more when a higher-ranking officer wasn't around.

Mr. Elliot stood and shook hands with Hodgins. "Is Miss Dickson in some sort of trouble?

"No, not at all." Hodgins gestured to two chairs in front of the big oak desk. "May we?"

"Of course. Forgive my manners."

The men waited until Miss Dickson was seated before taking their chairs. The office wasn't large, and the desk took up a lot of the room. Two file cabinets stood against the far wall, a single lantern on top of each one. Nothing frivolous took up residence in the office. Not even one painting hung on the wall.

"I'm afraid I have some rather disturbing news. It's regarding Miss Jackson."

"Yes, I understand she's not well. Has she taken a turn for the worse?"

"There's no easy way to say this. I'm afraid she's succumbed to her illness."

"No!" Miss Dickson gasped, began sobbing, then fainted, slipping towards the edge of the chair.

"Stokes!" Mr. Elliot bellowed for his clerk as Hodgins reached for Miss Dickson.

The door opened. "Sir?"

"Water for Miss Dickson."

Stokes glanced at the slumped woman, made a hasty exit, then quickly returned with a glass of water, as well as a damp cloth.

"Fetch a cab and have someone escort her home." Mr. Elliot stood beside Gertie, looking concerned and helpless, patting her limp hand repeatedly.

"Right away, sir."

Hodgins placed the damp cloth on Miss Dickson's forehead. "I took the liberty of having my constable inform your staff."

"Thank you. Not something I'd look forward to. I'm certain they'll all be quite upset. Everyone was very fond of her. I've never had an employee die before. Do you know what she perished from?"

"Unofficially, it looks like suicide, but I'd prefer it if you kept that to yourself until we confirm."

His eyes widened. "Good God. Why? She seemed to enjoy her work. Always smiling and laughing."

The look of shock seemed genuine. Hodgins had seen too many employers take the death of staff as a personal inconvenience.

"Yes. The owner of the boarding house where Misses Jackson and Dickson live couldn't believe it either." The detective pulled out his little book. "Is there anyone here she was close to? Beside Miss Dickson?"

He shrugged. "Sorry. I don't really know much about my employees' personal lives. Several of the men are married with families. Whether Misses Dickson and Jackson saw the single men outside business, I really couldn't say."

Gertie moaned. Her eyelids fluttered, then opened. The detective handed her the glass of water.

She took the glass but didn't drink. "Is Annabel really dead? I didn't realize she was that ill." She sat up straight, removing the damp cloth from her forehead. Gertie finally took a sip of water, then placed the glass and cloth on the desk.

Hodgins turned to face her. "Miss Dickson, I had hoped you could answer a few questions, but it can wait until you've recovered from the shock."

A knock on the door announced Stokes, who stepped in. "Carriage is here. Mr. Humphries will accompany her." He escorted her out and closed the office door.

Hodgins stood and extended his hand to the owner. "Thank you for your time. I'll leave you to attend to your staff."

"Please let me know when the service is. I'll have Stokes send flowers."

Hodgins nodded and found his constable chatting with the employees out front. He waved for him to leave and hailed a cab.

They settled in and Harrington flipped through his notebook. "I found out a few things, sir. Seems like Miss Jackson regularly had dinner with a few of the gentlemen here. I've got their names and addresses. Everyone was shocked when they heard she'd died."

"Good work." Hodgins took the letter from Miss Jackson's room out of his pocket. "Return address looks like it might be from her brother. He lives up in the Village of King. I'll go find him tomorrow. Hopefully, Stonehouse has a definitive answer as to her cause of death." He put the letter back in his pocket. "I'll read it at the station. We're almost there."

* * *

Shortly before Hodgins went home, Stonehouse knocked on the detective's office door. When he settled in the chair in front of Hodgins' desk, the doctor's brow was furrowed. He wasn't in his usual cheery mood.

"Problem, Doctor?"

"Puzzled, more like. Found something unusual in her stomach. Quicksilver. The medicine left in the bottle had no quicksilver in it, so I don't know where it came from. If she killed herself, the substance had to be in some type of container. What happened to the other bottle?"

"Interesting. There didn't appear to be a second bottle when I looked, unless it was hidden or tossed out. So, suicide, accident, or murder?"

"Suspicious? Unconfirmed? Haven't decided what to put on the death certificate. I can't say either, for certain. The liquid in the bottle was for simple nausea. The only thing I can say for certain is she's been dead at least twelve to fifteen hours. And no, she wasn't in the family way. Many young, unmarried women are so ashamed of their unexpected condition they end their life."

Hodgins leaned back. "Someone must have given her the poison late yesterday afternoon or early evening. Mrs. Holiwell said the doctor came last night, but didn't mention anyone else visiting. I'll check with her again to see if any of her guests had callers. If not, the only people who could have given her the poison would be the boarders and the landlady."

Stonehouse stood. "Don't envy you trying to figure it out."

CHAPTER TWO

Next morning, Hodgins arrived at work early, as did his constables. He asked Barnes and Harrington to find out what they could about Doctor Coward. "Harrington, go through reports and see if you can find any complaints." In response to the groan from the constable, he told him only the last six months.

"Barnes, ask Doctor Stonehouse if he's found out anything about Coward. Check into his license, schooling, that type of thing."

"Yes, sir. Oh, I spoke to Councilman Smith. He doesn't want to press charges against Nell. He's putting his name in to run again. Doesn't want the publicity."

Hodgins smiled. "Figured as much." He pulled out his pocket watch. It read 7:10. "Got a train to catch." Assignments given, he headed to Union Station to catch the first train to the Village of King.

The hour and a half ride up to King gave Hodgins time to think about Miss Jackson without interruptions. His constables had only spoken to a few people, but not one could come up with a reason she'd kill herself. *Where did the poison come from? I wonder… Would she have had enough time to take it and dispose of the bottle?*

Once he arrived at the little village, he recalled the map they had at the police station. The post office sat up the road north of the train station. The letter from Samuel to his sister had a return address simply listed as the post office in King. He'd need directions to the Jackson place, so he headed north.

Hodgins stood in line behind a woman picking up her mail, along with the local gossip.

The postmaster noticed Hodgins and cut the woman off as soon as she took a breath. "Got another customer, Mrs. Fielding. Have to chat later."

She turned and gave the detective the once over. "A stranger in a fancy suit. Must be lost. Can't farm dressed like that." She wrinkled her nose, stepped away from the counter, lingering a few feet away, remaining in earshot.

The postmaster smiled. "Can't imagine what a businessman like yourself would need in our little village. Step off the train to send a letter?"

"No. I'm looking for someone." Hodgins opened his jacket to show his badge. "Know where I might find Samuel Jackson?"

"He's not in any trouble, is he? Pretty quiet fella. Keeps to himself mostly."

Mrs. Fielding stepped closer, possibly to hear better.

"Family matter. If you'd be good enough to direct me?"

"Certainly, Detective."

Mrs. Fielding gasped and hurried out the door.

The postmaster looked embarrassed. "Won't be long before the entire village knows a detective is asking about Sam. Sorry 'bout that. Just follow the road west. Second farm."

"Thank you. Since people will no doubt be spreading all sorts about Mr. Jackson, let them know there's nothing nefarious in my visit. Just delivering news. No need to tarnish his reputation."

Hodgins left the postmaster to wonder about the news, exiting the post office to follow the road west. He noticed Mrs. Fielding pointing in his direction while speaking with another resident. He tipped his hat and continued to the corner, past the only store in town. Ten minutes later, he walked up the second laneway. *Better be the right farm.*

A small herd of dairy cattle grazed in the field to the east of the lane. The west field looked to be a small orchard. At the top of the lane, he spotted the farmhouse. A simple two-story structure too small for a large family. A gig with a chestnut horse tied to the porch road stood near the steps.

Hodgins walked up to the house and wiped the sweat from his brow before knocking on the screen door. The inside door sat open, allowing the slight breeze to enter the house. A woman approached from the back of the dwelling.

"Good morning, sir. How can I help you?" A woman in her early thirties smiled, but didn't open the screen door.

Hodgins removed his homburg. "Good morning. Is this the residence of Samuel Jackson?"

"Yes. I'm his fiancée. Sam is in the barn. I'll call him in." She came out and walked to a small wrought iron bell fastened to the side of the house with a matching bracket. "He'll be expecting a meal, I suppose." She giggled and rang the bell several times. Even though the bell was small, the tone was sufficient to carry a good distance in the quiet of the country side. "Should be here any time. Lemonade?"

"That would be welcome. Thank you."

"Come in out of the sun. Please excuse the mess. I'm trying to make the house homey. The wedding is only a few months away."

Fabric sat draped over the back of the sofa, and a sewing machine nestled by a side window in the sun.

"Looks like you're making curtains. My wife did that when we moved." He followed her through the house into the kitchen.

"May as well sit here at the table. Sammy will likely come in the back door." She looked out of the window. "He's coming now." She poured three glasses of lemonade and placed them on the table.

"Thank you, Miss…?"

She blushed. "Gracious. I never introduced myself. Claire Sawyer."

Hodgins smiled. "I'm guilty of the same thing. Detective Hodgins. Toronto Constabulary."

Mr. Jackson came in the back door as Hodgins introduced himself. "A detective from the city?" He looked at Claire. "Guess this means you didn't ring me in for lunch? Got yourself in a spot of bother?" His eyes twinkled. "He hasn't come to arrest you, has he?"

Hodgins took a gulp of lemonade before speaking. "It's you I've come to see, Mr. Jackson. I'm glad you have someone here with you. I've got bad news. There's no easy way to say this. Your sister has passed away. Circumstances are… suspicious."

Miss Sawyer gasped, almost dropping the pitcher still in her hand. "Belle? No. It can't be." She began to swoon, but caught herself before fainting.

Samuel got up and helped her to a chair, placing the glass pitcher on the table. He stood behind her, one hand on her shoulder. Jackson took a moment to take in the news.

"What do you mean, suspicious? I received a letter from her just a few days ago saying she felt unwell. Was that what she died of?"

"No. The coroner found quicksilver, mercury, in her system. We can't figure out where it came from. We originally thought suicide—"

"No! Never!" Samuel beat his fists on the arms of the chair. "She had no reason."

Claire slumped in the chair, colour draining from her face.

Samuel reached for her before she slid off. "Forgive the outburst, Detective. It is rather much to take in. We haven't had a visit from Annabel for a few months, but she was in good spirits. Her correspondence cheery."

Claire wept, hands covering her face, raising her head briefly when Samuel mentioned Belle's last visit.

"I've ruled suicide out. As you said, we haven't found any reason, and we didn't find any poison in her room. Everyone we spoke to said she was happy."

Claire sniffled. "She was to be my maid of honour."

"Do you know if she had a beau?"

She smiled. "Several. Belle was never short of an escort. No one special. She wasn't ready to marry and raise a family. Quite enjoyed her independence."

Hodgins removed the notebook from his jacket pocket and sat it on the table. "Is there anyone you can think of who held a grudge, or was jealous?"

Claire opened her mouth to speak, but changed her mind when Samuel touched her arm.

Both shrugged and shook their heads.

Hodgins made a few brief notes and stood. "If you think of anything, please contact me at Station House Four, Toronto. I'm very sorry for your loss. I'll keep you informed of our progress."

All the way home, Hodgins couldn't shake the feeling they were hiding something. He tried to put it down to shock and grief, but that one look from Claire said otherwise.

When the train pulled into Union Station, Hodgins hurried to the police station.

Barnes followed the detective into his office. "Sir, we've come up empty on Doctor Coward. Not much known about him. He didn't attend school here at the College of Physicians and Surgeons of Ontario, so I've sent a telegram to the Montreal Medical Institute, the as well as Dalhousie College in Nova Scotia. It's possible he's not even from Canada.

"Harrington couldn't find a complaint against him either, so he's going through *The Globe* to see if there are any write-ups mentioning him. He hasn't come across anything on the doctor, but there's an article on another young woman in her early twenties who died shortly after taking medicine for a minor ailment. The physician was Doctor Traybar. I can't find any listing for his practice, either."

"Probably nothing other than a coincidence. People get sick and die unexpectedly. Shame it's someone so young, but it happens. Was there anything in the write-up indicating anything unusual?"

Barnes shook his head. "No, nothing strange except I can't locate the doctor."

"He may simply have moved. Keep looking. I have a feeling foul play is involved." Hodgins waved a hand at the empty chair in front of his desk. "Sit, Henry. Update me on Riddell. I understand his eye has completely healed, but he's not been as lucky with his foot."

Barnes leaned back in the chair. "That beating last fall really took a lot out of him. His mind, I mean, He's really depressed. Feels useless."

"I can't believe the bones haven't healed. It's been almost six months."

"They've healed as much as they're going to. Tom said he'll have a permanent limp. He's been meaning to come in to talk to you, but is too embarrassed."

"Nonsense. His injury is simply a battle scar. Something to be proud of. I'll have to make time to visit him, and have that chat with the Chief Inspector about Tom coming back. Should have done that months ago. I did promise his job will be waiting when he's ready to return. If it's just the limp stopping him, we'll have to remind him of the scar on the Chief Inspector's face. May as well see if the Chief's available."

Barnes nodded. "Tom would enjoy a visit from you. If he has a job to come back to, maybe it'll perk him up."

Hodgins stood. "Maybe it was just being cooped up over winter that's got Tom down. Get him out in the fresh spring air. Do him a world of good."

Barnes moved to the doorway and stopped. "I've convinced him to dine with Violet and me on Saturday. She's got it into her head Tom needs a wife, only he doesn't know it yet. Lined up one of her friends to join us as a surprise. I just hope he takes it well." Barnes chuckled and grinned his usual lop-sided smile. "Fingers crossed."

* * *

After talking to the Chief Inspector, Hodgins stopped to visit Riddell, hoping he'd be able to return to work soon. Mrs. Riddell led the detective to the back yard where the recuperating constable pulled weeds from the vegetable garden.

"Hello, Tom. I see your mother's put you to good use. Are you ready to return to work? I've had a word with the Chief Inspector, and you can return any time."

Riddell stood, brushing the dirt from his trousers. "Well, I'm not certain, sir. My eye has healed fine, but my leg will never be the same. Can't be a copper if I'm deformed."

"Deformed? Nonsense. A little limp won't prevent you from working. If you can't handle walking the beat all day, I've got an idea for that. As for this so-call deformity, think of it as a good tale to tell. A battle would. The chief certainly doesn't hesitate to tell people all about how he got that scar on his face."

"Yes, I've heard that many times. But a bum leg isn't the same as a scar."

Hodgins placed a hand on Tom's shoulder. "Like I said, I've got something in mind. Give it a think. Talk it over with your mother. If you're up to it, come in tomorrow."

Heading home, Hodgins whistled as he walked. He enjoyed the bit of daylight that lingered as the season changed. Many trees along the roadside sported the light green of fresh growth. *Won't be long until all the trees are covered in new leaves.*

As usual, Scraps enthusiastically greeted him at the front door. Hodgins grabbed the leash and walked the dog around the block, stopping so he could have a good run around the yard at Ketchum school. By the time they returned home, the pooch was ready for a nap.

After dinner, Sara took Holly and Ivy into the backyard, watched over by Scraps. The former stray had turned into an excellent watchdog for the children. Hodgins and his wife, Cordelia, sat at the kitchen table enjoying a quiet cup of tea.

"I think it's time to start planning a party." Cordelia set her teacup down and smiled at her husband.

"What brought that on so suddenly?"

"It's the twins' third birthday in a couple of weeks, and the first anniversary of their adoption. We can set up a cold buffet in the yard, if the weather is nice. They're too young to have their own friends, but Sara can invite her classmates and their younger siblings, and we can have our friends and family over. My parents don't get out much any longer, so it will be a nice treat for them. They've slowed down so much. And we haven't had your brother and his family over since Christmas."

Hodgins took a long sip. "It's hard to imagine the twins were adopted. With their red hair, anyone would believe you were their natural mother. You know, a party sounds like a great idea. I can invite my constables, and Stonehouse, too."

"Yes, and the good doctor will no doubt bring Amelia. They've been keeping regular company ever since she helped when that family was attacked last fall. Oh, I almost forgot. She's had another vision of a child being kidnapped."

"Afraid I can't start any investigation based on a vision. Besides, I've got my hands full with the death of a young woman. Stonehouse found quicksilver in her system. Said it was in most of her organs."

Cordelia gasped. "How horrid! Did she take it on purpose?"

"Can't tell." Hodgins sighed. "The medicine bottle found in her room had no traces. If she took it intentionally, I don't know how. There were no other bottles in her room."

Cordelia refilled their cups. "Could someone have found her, removed the poison to hide the suicide, then waited until someone else found her?"

"Hmm. Hadn't thought of that. Peculiar thing for a person to do. No doubt I would have thought of it eventually." He winked at his wife. "First thing in the morning, I'll send one of the lads to search the boarding house rooms and trash, just in case. As usual, you've thought of something helpful." Hodgins glanced out the window. "It's beginning to get rather dark. I'll bring the children in and have Sara help put the twins to bed."

* * *

When Hodgins arrived at the station house, Riddell sat at his old desk, chatting with Barnes and Harrington. Barnes noticed the detective and nodded towards Riddell. "Look who's finally decided to come to work. We're just trying to decide whose paperwork he should do first." He gave Riddell a gentle slap on the back.

"You'll all do your own paperwork. Tom will be busy with his own cases, and I want you to teach him how to use the new photographic equipment. Now, I've got a job for you two."

Hodgins sent both Barnes and Riddell to the boarding house to search for discarded or hidden bottles. An hour later, they returned empty-handed.

"No luck then?" the detective asked.

"Maybe." Barnes stood in front of Hodgins' desk. "We found a few medicine bottles in the trash bin and left them with Doctor Stonehouse. He's going to analyze the contents right away. They didn't smell funny. Then again, I don't know what quicksilver smells like."

"Don't believe it has a scent. Good work." Hodgins glanced over Barnes' shoulder. "What's Harrington up to?"

"Still trying to track down the doctor that attended Miss Jackson."

"Found him!" Harrington's voice rang through the station. He gathered up the newspaper and ran to Hodgins' office. "There's a small ad for his practice."

The detective read the ad. "Mill Street. Near the docks. Not an ideal place to set up a practice. Does make for a quick get-a-way, though. Harrington, why don't you accompany me, seeing as you found it? Barnes, you wait for the doctor's report. Hopefully, he has something by the time we return. While you're waiting, show Tom how to use the photographic equipment."

The detective and Harrington walked to the corner to wait for the horse-drawn trolly which would deposit them within a few blocks of their destination.

A short ride later, luck was with them as a man approached from the opposite direction, stopping at the doctor's office ahead of them. Hodgins called out as the man unlocked the door.

"Are you Doctor Coward?"

"Yes. Come into my office. What seems to be the problem?" He glanced at the uniformed constable. "One of your officers ill?"

"This isn't a medical call." Hodgins introduced himself and the constable. "I've been told you attended a patient at the ladies' boarding house on John Street two days ago. Miss Jackson?"

"Yes. She's one of my patients. Has she taken ill again?"

"You've not been informed? They found her dead the next morning. Can you tell me the nature of her illness?"

"Dead, you say? Tragic. So young. She had a simple stomach ailment. Not at all serious, just uncomfortable for her. Nausea, cramps. That sort of thing. How did she die?"

"The coroner found quicksilver during the autopsy. A lot of it. Not something one would expect for a stomach ailment."

Coward puffed out his chest. "Wait. You're not suggesting I gave her the mercury? I'll have you know I prepared the medicine myself. I can assure you I put no mercury, or quicksilver as you call it, into the bottle."

Hodgins held up his hands. "No. I can assure you no blame is being cast. The doctor analyzed the contents of the bottle and it didn't contain any of the poison. Can you tell me about her frame of mind? Did she confide any problems? Some reason she may have been depressed?"

Coward raised an eyebrow. "Are you suggesting suicide? Strange way to go about it."

"Where would she obtain it? Is it readily available?"

"Beauty products, Detective. They can be most deadly. Some women use mercury to thin eyebrows. Someone can easily purchase small quantities at an apothecary." He paused. "It's also used to cure syphilis." He cleared his throat. "I can assure you that was not the case with Miss Jackson."

"Thank you for your time, doctor."

As they walked back to catch the trolly, Harrington nervously asked a question. "Uh, sir? Have you forgotten Miss Jackson worked at a pharmaceutical company?"

Hodgins laughed at the constable's shaky voice. "No, I haven't forgotten. And don't be afraid to remind me of the obvious. I fully intend checking their records. They're expected to maintain meticulous accounts of quantities used and purchased. I found no cosmetics in Miss Jackson's room, except simple face cream. Same stuff my wife uses. May as well check at the pharmacy now. Catch them off guard."

CHAPTER THREE

When they arrived at Elliot's, all eyes were on them, hoping for information. "Detective, have you news?" One of the men questioned previously seemed anxious to know.

"No. Afraid not. I need to see your records. Specifically, for quicksilver."

"Certainly. I'll fetch Mr. Elliot. He keeps the log books in his office." The clerk hurried into the back to see if his employer was available.

Five minutes later, Elliot called Hodgins into his office, Harrington close behind.

"I understand you want to see my log books. Is this regarding Miss Jackson's death? She died from quicksilver? Ghastly. I can assure you, everything is in order." Elliot's hand shook as he handed a piece of paper to the detective. "The report from the authorities, done just last month." He clasped his hands behind his back to hide the shakes. "The death of Miss Jackson has me rattled. Just the thought the poison may have come from here, well… you can understand."

Hodgins glanced at the report. "Yes, I'm certain your records are in order. However, seeing as how your employee died just the other day, I'll need to see something more current."

Elliot opened his mouth to respond, but hesitated. Hodgins watched as the information rattled around the pharmacist's brain. "Are you thinking Miss Jackson stole a quantity with plans to take her own life?"

"We can't rule it out. I understand she's kept company with more than one of your employees. Do they all have access to the quicksilver?"

Elliot took a deep breath and nodded. "Suicide or a jealous suitor? I trust all my employees, but one never truly knows what goes on in another's head." He got up, crossed the room to one of the filing cabinets, and removed a large ledger book. "This is what you need. Each person responsible for the mixtures keeps his own daily record. At the end of the day, they're brought in here, and I personally enter them in the master ledger. Once it's all tallied, I check the inventory to ensure it balances. There may be a slight discrepancy due to spillage, but I guarantee the difference is minimal and recorded. Maybe only a couple of grams by month end. Usually far less."

The detective took the ledger and reviewed the entries for the past several weeks, noting the current inventory amount. He handed the ledger back. "Your records are immaculate. Would you show me the inventory now? I need to confirm everything so I can eliminate this line of inquiry."

"This way." Elliot led the detective and constable to the back, where shelves of various powders and liquids were stored. "It's right… oh, one of the fellows must have it."

They turned to exit when an employee came in. Hodgins recognized him as the one who approached when he first arrived.

"Sorry to interrupt. Just returning the quicksilver."

"Thank you, Jacob. How much has been used today? The detective needs an accurate account."

"Two of us used it, Mr. Elliot."

"Gather the dailies. I'll measure this and be right out."

Hodgins watched closely as Elliot weighted the bottle and contents after Jacob returned.

The pharmacist explained as he made calculations and included the amounts on the dailies from Jacob. "Each bottle's weight is recorded. A simple matter of deducting that from the total weight. If I poured the contents out, minuscule amounts may cling to the bottle and scale, or spill out. I dispose of all spillage to keep the supply pure."

Once the calculations were completed, the discrepancy was less than an eighth of a gram. Elliot led the detective back to his office.

"I believe you also have a factory and warehouse? I'd like to check there as well."

Elliot stopped by Stokes' desk and blinked several times. "Yes, I have other premises. Is it necessary to check them?"

"Afraid so. According to the city directory, your factory runs from 20 to 28 Beverley Street and the warehouse is on Front Street East."

The pharmacist nodded, wiping sweat from his brow. "The warehouse is simply a room in a much larger building. I don't keep any pharmaceuticals there. Only bottles and the like. Just basic non-medicinal supplies. Stokes can show you." He took a key off a small keyring and handed it to his assistant. "May as well start at the wareroom. Only two buildings over. Stokes will introduce you to my son at the factory. He's scheduled to be there all day. Afraid I'll need Stokes to come back right away."

Elliot confirmed his instructions with Stokes. "Bring back the key before you go to the factory. Tell my son to cooperate fully."

"Of course, sir." The trio dodged buggies and horse droppings as the assistant led the officers to the room at 3 Front Street East and unlocked the door. The room had no windows, so Stokes lit a small lantern sitting on a table by the door. "As you can see, it's mostly supplies and old equipment storage."

Hodgins took the lantern and walked around. Harrington remained at the doorway with Stokes, towering over him. The detective ran a finger across a small crate. "Quite dusty. Don't suppose you come in often."

"Only when we need more bottles, corks, that sort of thing." Stokes pointed across the room. "Or to store old equipment. That scale's been broken for almost a year, but Mr. Elliot insists on keeping it."

Hodgins grinned. "My father was like that. 'Never know when it'll come in handy.' He said that at least once a week. I'm satisfied there's nothing of interest here. Harrington, you may as well go back to the station. See if Barnes needs any help. Otherwise, make your rounds. I'll go to the factory and speak to the son."

While he waited for Stokes to return the key to his employer, Hodgins hailed a passing hansom. The factory wasn't far, but it would cut their time in half. Fifteen minutes later, Hodgins sat in a small grimy office with the young Mr. Elliot. Not at all like the office his father had at the pharmacy.

"My father mentioned the death of one of his female employees. I only knew Miss Jackson in passing, so I doubt I can provide you with any pertinent information."

Hodgins leaned back and crossed his long legs. "It's not information on Miss Jackson I require. Just need to confirm you aren't missing any quicksilver."

"Good Lord! Is that what killed her? We do mix it with some of our goods. Mostly in beauty products sold at the pharmacy. Rarely in anything else. The records here are even more meticulous than that of my father's, as the factory is a much larger enterprise than the small mixtures made by him at the store."

Elliot brought out the ledgers and allowed Hodgins time to review everything.

"As you said, the records here are meticulous. The difference due to spillage is even less than at the store. Impressive. As this was just updated yesterday, I don't believe I'll have to check your inventory. Quantities would have been taken much earlier." Hodgins handed the ledger back. "Thank you for your time. I'll speak with the coroner, but I believe more than your difference and your father's combined was found in her stomach."

After leaving the factory, Hodgins purchased a meat pie from a street vendor, then stopped to see Doctor

Stonehouse to confirm the amount of quicksilver from Elliot's calculation was insufficient to kill Miss Jackson.

"Less than an eighth of a gram? That would certainly make her a little ill, but nothing that would kill her."

"That's what I thought. I guess I've eliminated one possible source." Hodgins stroked his moustache as he thought.

Stonehouse leaned against his desk. "Well, it's enough if consumed regularly. An eighth of a gram every day or two would build up over time. But you said she'd only been ill a few days. There's too much in her organs for a slow poisoning. It was likely given in one dose, shortly before death."

Hodgins let out a soft breath. "So, she was murdered. And it had to be someone who either lived at her lodgings, or visited recently. Thank you, Doctor." Hodgins smiled. "Not sure if you made my job easier or more difficult. Before I forget, Delia would like you and Amelia to dine with us again soon. Twin's party doesn't count."

"Certainly." He gestured at two additional covered bodies on his tables. "Little busy at the moment, but soon."

Hodgins strolled back to the station house, deep in thought. Inside, newspapers lay strewn across Barnes' desks. "What're you up to?"

"Thought I'd look for another ad for that doctor. Maybe look into him a little more. He's only been renting there a month."

"Don't waste too much time on it. I want you to go back and gather Miss Jackson's beauty products and toiletries. There aren't many. It's possible someone put quicksilver in one of them. I believe it can be absorbed through the skin."

They were interrupted when the front door to the station opened, banging against the wall. A man came in shouting, a wailing woman trailing behind. All heads turned. "Our baby has been taken!"

Hodgins hurried over and led them into his office, motioning for Barnes to bring tea. The detective shut his door to give them privacy. While he waited for the couple to settle and were able to speak coherently, he quietly assessed them. The gentleman was well dressed, a sign of some degree of wealth. His wife wore a fur stole around her shoulders, despite the pleasant May weather. *Must have money.* It took a few minutes, but he finally got their names. Mr. and Mrs. Otis Throckmorton. Hodgins almost dropped his pencil. They had adopted the younger brother of his twins. The baby had been taken from his imprisoned mother, Mrs. Brown, immediately after birth. Since she would never be released, the child was put in care until adopted.

He composed himself and began with his questions. "Have you noticed anyone hanging around recently? Someone who had no business dealings in the neighbourhood?"

Throckmorton shook his head. "No. No one I've seen."

His wife, Cassandra, stopped sobbing and placed a hand on her husband's arms. "There was a man a few days ago. A tramp, I believe. When I opened the door, he ran off."

Hodgins sat, pencil poised. "Can you describe him? I don't believe it was a tramp. They generally go to neighbourhoods looking for work in exchange for food. Not likely he'd run off when a door opened."

Throckmorton covered his wife's hand with his and addressed Hodgins. "Are you implying this man may have been checking out our house? Trying to get a feel for our habits so he could take the baby?"

Mrs. Throckmorton gasped. "A kidnapper?"

"Yes, possibly." Hodgins tapped his pencil against his notebook. "Or likely someone hired. What did he look like? Anything distinguishable about him? Facial hair? A mole? A limp?"

"He wasn't close enough for me to see his face, but I believe he may have been in his thirties. Difficult to tell under that beard. And he ran off quick, so I don't think he had any issues with his legs."

Hodgins wrote down her comments. "When was this?"

She thought for a moment. "It was the same day I attended the temperance meeting. Tuesday."

Hodgins suppressed a chuckle. His wife, Cordelia, had attended one of those meetings a few months back. When she returned home, she declared the ladies to be a pack of humourless biddies, wanting nothing more than to make all men miserable.

"If this was a kidnapping, there should be a ransom note. Have you the means to pay?" Hodgins glanced up from jotting his notes, already expecting a yes.

Throckmorton nodded. "I own several businesses and properties. I can pay."

The detective made another note. "I'll have my men interview your neighbours. Someone may have noticed him, too. Where was the baby taken from? Was there a note?"

"No. No note. My wife was in the nursery with the baby, and went down to the kitchen for some lemonade. When she went back up, Alfie was gone. We named him Alfred, after Alfred the Great."

His wife burst into tears, blubbering. "It's my fault. All my fault."

"Give me your address, then take your wife home. We'll check the area right away."

As soon as they left, Hodgins called Barnes, Riddell, and Harrington into his office. "Something's come up that takes priority over Miss Jackson's death. A baby's been taken right out of the family home."

The constables stared, mouths open.

Harrington finally spoke. "Why would someone steal a baby? Is the family rich? Have they been asked to pay a ransom?"

Hodgins shook his head. "No ransom demand. Not yet, anyway. The family is well off, but not rich. Riddell, do you feel able to walk the neighbourhood?"

"Yes, I can manage several blocks before my foot begins to throb. I'm just glad my eye healed. Quite enjoying learning photography and developing the images so I can be of some use."

"Why don't you come to the house with me and Barnes to take photographs of the yard and nursery? That's where the baby was taken from. Maybe we'll find footprints or something under the window."

Barnes spoke up. "Remember the girl killed on Duchess Street? Olive. We found a piece of torn shirt on the fence."

Hodgins pointed at Barnes. "Exactly. Now, we need to take pictures before we collect any evidence. Camera might pick up something small we missed." He nodded, satisfied things would be done in the correct order. "So, that's settled. Harrington, you check every house on and around Strachan to see if anyone saw a man hanging around on Tuesday. In his thirties, with a beard. And if anyone saw him more recently. Riddell, gather the photographic equipment. I'll go round to John Mitchell's livery and hire a buggy. Be ready in twenty minutes."

As Hodgins walked to Mitchell's, he thought about his twins and the missing baby. He hadn't told Cordelia he knew who adopted the convicted woman's baby. *Had the new parents been told about the child's parents?* Before he was born, they'd discussed adopting him so the twins would know their baby brother. Unfortunately, even with their nanny, Beryl, and daughter Sara, three children under the age of three would be too much for them to manage. *Better tell Delia soon, before it hits the newspaper.*

While he knew all about the baby's background, he didn't get the impression the Throckmorton's had been told about the twin sisters little Alfie had. *What reason would anyone have for taking the baby? Money doesn't appear to be the reason, yet.*

Hodgins arrived at the livery and, after a brief chat with Mitchell, headed back to Station Four, driving a well-used landau. His constables waited on the front step.

Barnes whistled. "A landau. We're going in style."

Harrington nudged him. "Take another look. She's not in the best condition."

Hodgins raised his hands, ready to flick the reins and get the horses moving again. "Would you rather walk? John bought it recently, after the owner had an accident. Too costly to repair, so he got a good bargain. Fixed it himself. Once he paints it and repairs the folding top, he'll rent it out for a pretty penny. We're good as long as it doesn't rain."

Barnes climbed in first and took the camera equipment so Riddell could get in. Harrington reached over to help the injured lad, but was waved off. The three constables were barely settled when the horse took off. Hodgins chuckled as his passengers grabbed hold and grumbled.

When they arrived at the Throckmorton home, a carriage sat at the curb. "Do you think they have company?" Barnes gave the fancy carriage a once-over as he assisted Riddell with the equipment again.

"Could be a family member come to offer comfort. Harrington, you may as well call next door and go from there." Hodgins started up the walk. "Only one way to find out who's here."

A woman answered the door, at least ten years older than the distraught mother who'd come to the station to report the kidnapping.

"Detective Hodgins, ma'am. We need to take photographs and search for anything that might point to whoever did this."

She stared down her long, wide nose at the trio. "My sister-in-law is very upset. You'll have to come back another day." She began to close the door, but Hodgins pushed back.

"I understand. I have three children myself. If we don't start immediately, all clues may be lost."

A male voice sounded from the room to the left. "Let them in, Beulah. They have a job to do, and we'd like our son back."

Mr. Throckmorton stepped out of the room and allowed Hodgins and the two constables in. Soft sobbing alerted the detective to the presence of the distraught mother. *Wonder why they didn't call a doctor to give her something?*

"Excuse my sister. We're all terribly upset." He turned to Beulah. "Ask cook to send a tray of tea to the sitting room."

"No tea for us. Thank you for the offer. If you wouldn't mind showing us where Alfie was taken from?"

"Yes. Upstairs."

Hodgins went up behind Throckmorton, indicating for Barnes and Riddell to follow. He'd only made it to the second step when a loud crash came from behind. The tripod and a small side table lay on the floor. Barnes hugged a decorative fish-covered bowl in one arm, bellows camera in the other.

Throckmorton glanced at the bowl Barnes protected. "A Lycett. Never cared for it. The nursery is this way." He continued climbing the stairs.

Riddell untangled the tripod from his crutches. Beulah took the bowl, glaring at Barnes. The constables hurried to catch up.

"That's the nursery." He pointed to the doorway at the end of the hall. "Neither of us has been able to go back in. Please, you have to find my son."

"We'll do everything possible. Wait for us downstairs with your wife."

When the gentleman left, Hodgins scolded the constables. "If you can't control the equipment, I'll have to find someone who can. You're lucky that bowl didn't break. Could very easily have been something priceless."

"Yes, sir."

"Sorry, sir."

"Right. Get that thing set up and start taking pictures." Hodgins walked to the window. "Start here."

A large maple tree grew near the house. One substantial branch passed in font of the window. The constables joined him, Barnes still holding the camera, while Riddell got the tripod set up, using it for support as he'd propped his crutches by the doorway.

Barnes leaned out the open window. "Looks strong enough to hold any size man. Do you think that's how he got in?"

"The window's wide open. All he'd have to do is climb in and place the baby in a satchel, then lower him down on a rope. Take a picture." The detective stepped aside so Riddell could get the window and branch in the viewfinder.

While Riddell took pictures around the room, Hodgins and Barnes searched. Hodgins stopped in front of a small chest of drawers and called to Riddell. "Get a picture of this. One of the drawers is open and empty. Could be something or nothing."

They spent thirty minutes searching the nursery before heading back down. "Put that equipment in the landau and wait for me. Barnes, see where Harrington is." Hodgins opened the front door, grinning when he noticed the bowl had yet to be put back on the table. *Don't blame her for waiting for us to leave.* He closed the door after his men exited, then joined the bereft couple.

"A few questions. You said you haven't been in the nursery since you discovered Alfie missing. Has anyone else in the household been in there? Your sister perhaps?"

Throckmorton shook his head. "No one has gone in. Beulah only arrived a little before you, and hasn't been upstairs. I have given the cook and maid instructions not to enter."

"I'd like to confirm that." Hodgins faced Beulah. "Is it correct you haven't been upstairs?"

She maintained the same hard look as when she answered the door. "That is correct. Well, not in the nursery. I went up to fetch a day jacket for my sister-in-law. Didn't go near the baby's room."

"Thank you. Are the maid and cook the only other ones in the house? I'll need to speak with them."

Beulah rose. "I'll get them."

"I'd like to speak with them in private."

Beulah looked at her brother, who nodded.

"I'll take you to the kitchen. Maid's probably taking tea with cook." She led him to the back of the house, then re-joined her brother.

"Yer here 'bout the sprog what was took, ain't ya?" A young girl wearing a maid's cap sat at the table with a plump, older woman.

"That's right. Did either of you ladies see or hear anything out of the ordinary?"

The plump cook shook her head. "Don't have time to see much of anything outside the kitchen, 'sept when I go to market."

"I seen that feller hanging 'round. The day afore the baby was took." The maid sat up straighter, proud to have information for the detective.

"Can you describe him for me?" Hodgins had his notebook and pencil ready.

"Nah. Didn't get a good look. He scarpered off soon as he seed me looking." The maid took a scone off the plate in the centre of the table and smeared it with jam.

Hodgins sighed. "Have either of you been in the nursery? After you discovered him missing?"

Both shook their heads.

"You won't be in any trouble if you were. I just need to know the truth."

"We're telling you the truth. Honest." The maid looked at the cook, who agreed.

"Okay. Thank you."

Hodgins left the kitchen and stopped at the doorway of the sitting room to address the couple. "One final question for now. Was the window in the nursery open before Alfie was taken?"

"Yes." Mrs. Throckmorton sniffled. "Fresh air is important for a healthy baby."

"Is that how he was taken?" Mr. Throckmorton stood beside his wife, hand on her shoulder.

"Possibly. It's unlikely he came through the front door unnoticed. Not ruling anything out. I'll keep you informed of our findings. If you remember anything, please let me know."

CHAPTER FOUR

Hodgins joined the constables and headed back to the station house in the landau. A block away, they passed a wagon with a chest of drawers tied down. He pulled on the reins, stopping the horse. "Blast. Forgot to ask about the empty drawer." He hesitated, trying to decide what to do. "Could be nothing. It's getting late." He flicked the reins and continued on.

When they returned, Barnes headed to a small room in the back to develop the glass negatives, showing Riddell the process while Hodgins returned their ride.

When Hodgins returned, a man stood at the sergeant's desk, arguing about a fine. He scurried past and called to Harrington. "Floyd, come into my office and tell me what the neighbours had to say." The detective picked up his pencil to add any new information to his own notes.

"Afraid I don't have much." The constable didn't bother to open his notebook. "Seems no one saw a thing. The husbands were either at work or their clubs, wives taking care of the household, whatever that means. Servants busy cleaning and cooking. Oh, and no answer at the one across the street."

Hodgins threw the pencil down. It careened off the front of his desk. Harrington reached out and grabbed it before it hit the floor.

"Nice catch." Hodgins took it and set it on top of his notebook.

"Too bad we couldn't catch a break with the baby snatcher." Harrington shook his head and tsked. "Imagine someone stealing a little baby."

"It's early days. The people from the empty house will return eventually. Hopefully, they only just left and may have noticed the man hanging around. Why don't you head home? You can continue looking through the newspapers tomorrow. Maybe you'll find something relating to Miss Jackson. I'll check on Barnes."

The detective walked down the hall to the room where the plates were being developed. When they purchased the equipment, they cleared part of the storage room to make space. Eventually, it would be used strictly for developing photographs. A hastily written sign hung on the door, warning everyone to keep out. He knocked, calling out to Barnes.

"Still working, sir. Shouldn't be much longer."

"Fine. Go home when you're done. I'll look at them in the morning."

* * *

After supper, they put the twins to bed, and Sara sat in her room reviewing for a spelling test. Cordelia joined her husband in the sitting room, taking the chair by the fire, opposite Hodgins.

"New hairstyle, Delia? Quite fetching."

"Glad you finally noticed. Even though you've assured me your investments are doing well, I hesitate to spend too much. Tomorrow I plan on shopping for a new frock for the party. While I have your attention, can we discuss the party for Holly and Ivy? It's getting close and invitations need to be sent."

"Party? Oh, yes. Before we do that, I need to tell you something. I believe it relates to those visions Amelia claims to have." He shifted uncomfortably, trying to decide the best way to tell his wife the disconcerting secret he'd been keeping.

Delia leaned forward. "You mean the ones about a baby and us? You know whose baby it is?"

"Yes. I'm afraid I've been keeping something from you."

Delia gasped. "You don't mean you… a baby?" Her eyes watered.

"Good God, no! How could you think such a thing?" He chuckled. "Guess that makes my secret seem insignificant now. I know the name of the couple who have the twins' brother. Someone snatched the little boy today, right out of their home. It' bound to come out in the newspapers and I wanted you to hear it from me. I'm sorry I didn't tell you when I first found out." He chuckled. "Figured you'd bring up wishing you'd adopt him yourself."

"I don't know if I should feel relieved or upset." She dried her eyes. "Why would someone take the child? He'd be about a year old, wouldn't he?"

"Yes, that sounds right. We don't know why they want this baby specifically. No ransom has been demanded as yet." He raised an eyebrow. "You're not angry I didn't tell you about the boy's whereabouts?"

"No. I suspect you weren't supposed to find out and didn't want to involve me."

"It's not customary to divulge that information. Especially as we have his sisters. Could get messy and embarrassing if people tried to contact new parents when siblings have been separated."

"Yes, I can see that. But if I had a brother or sister, I'd want to know. Imagine if they ever met and fell in love?"

"Unthinkable. At some point, we'll have to decide whether or not to tell Holly and Ivy they have a brother. Years away yet."

"We may have to tell them sooner than we want. Sara knows Mrs. Brown was with child when arrested. It could slip out."

He nodded. "Yes. We'll talk to Sara sooner than we planned and make certain she understands she can't say anything until we're ready to tell the story. Now, about this party. What did you have in mind?"

* * *

Barnes beat Hodgins to work the next morning and had the prints ready to show the detective. He followed Hodgins into his office. "They came out quite well. Tom seems adept at both taking and developing them. Caught on to the process quicker than I did." Barnes spread the pictures across the desk.

Hodgins looked them over. "Very nice." He picked up two. "I'm going back there this morning." He waved one photograph. "This open drawer has me worried." He waved the other. "And this needs to be dealt with." He showed Barnes the picture of the open window. "That limb should be removed. It's an open invitation for thieves."

"What do you want us to do today? Baby or Miss Jackson?"

"For now, keep searching for anything about the doctor. Have you heard from the universities?"

"Just Dalhousie. Doctor Coward wasn't a student there. Doctor Stonehouse has also made inquires and hasn't found anything."

"One of you can look into the employees at Elliot's. Don't care who. Decide amongst yourselves, just don't have Riddell doing anything to aggravate his foot. I shouldn't be long."

Hodgins dug through his desk for an envelope to protect the pictures from the threat of rain, then started for the Throckmorton's. Even though it was just over an hour's walk, the weather was still nice, and it gave him time to think about both the kidnapping and the murdered woman.

Once again, Beulah answered the door.

"My brother isn't home, but he left instructions for us to answer any questions should you return. Make it quick." She led him into the sitting room. Her sister-in-law sat by the fireplace, staring at the flames.

"Cassandra, the police are here again."

She didn't respond.

Hodgins walked over and stood beside her. "Mrs. Throckmorton? Cassandra? I have a couple of photographs to show you. Could you tell me about them?"

Slowly, she turned her head. Her eyes were red and puffy.

He turned to Beulah. "Has she slept or eaten?"

"Barely. The doctor left laudanum, but she won't take it."

Kneeling beside the chair, he handed Cassandra the photo of the chest of drawers. "Is this drawer normally empty?"

She took the picture, but said nothing.

Hodgins turned to Beulah. "Do you know?"

She leaned over to look. "The baby's clothing is kept in those drawers, as far as I know."

The front door opened and closed, then Otis Throckmorton joined them in the sitting room. "Had business at the bank, just in case they demanded a ransom. Need to know how much money I can get quickly. Have you news?"

"No, nothing new." He gently released Cassandra's fingers from the picture and showed Otis. "Could you tell me exactly what you kept in this drawer?"

"Afraid not. Alice may know. The maid. She does the laundry and puts away everything." He nodded at his sister, indicating the doorway.

She understood his meaning. "I'll fetch her." Beulah returned a minute later, Alice close behind.

Hodgins smiled at the maid. "Would you accompany us upstairs and tell me what's missing from the drawer in the nursery?"

She looked to her employer as he'd given instructions not to enter that room.

The detective understood the look and answered for Otis. "It's all right. You can enter. We're finished with it."

Hodgins, Throckmorton, and Alice went up to the nursery, Throckmorton leading the way. The maid went through the drawers to see what remained.

"Looks like diapers, pins, a bonnet, and two, maybe three little outfits. All the blankets are gone. They were in the drawer what was left open."

"Thank you. That's all, Alice." Hodgins waited until the maid left, then turned to Throckmorton. "It's been two days and no ransom demand made. That, and the discovery the thief took some of the child's clothing, leads me to believe Alfie was stolen and not kidnapped."

Otis paled. "Stolen? You mean we won't get him back? Oh, Lord. How can I tell Cassandra?"

"We'll do our best to find the person who did this. Why was *your* baby taken? I mean, why Alfie specifically? I've heard babies crying in other houses along this street. That's what I need to find out."

They went back to the sitting room, immediately shushed by Beulah. "She's finally fallen asleep." She pointed at her sister-in-law, still sitting by the fireplace, head resting against the wing of the chair.

Hodgins gestured for Otis to join him in the hall. "Could you provide me with the names and addresses of any neighbour with small children?"

"You think he's tried this before?"

"Anything's possible. Oh, and I'd advise you to find someone to remove that branch crossing by the nursery window."

When the detective left, he had five homes to visit. Unfortunately, no one said they'd ever had reason to believe anyone attempted to take their child or break into the house. Puzzled, Hodgins returned to the station. He took one file from the cabinet and spread the contents across his desk and read and re-read the notes.

Ten minutes later, he raised his head when someone knocked. He waved Barnes in.

"Is something the matter, sir? You've been staring at your desk for a while."

"Just trying to figure out this puzzle with the baby. I believe they singled Alfie out." He explained his visit to Throckmorton's and the neighbours.

Barnes dropped onto the chair in front of the desk. "Maybe Alfie was taken simply because that branch made entry to the house easy?"

"No. A couple of the houses had their perambulator sitting on the front lawn under a tree, baby soundly sleeping. If you want to steal a baby, snatching one off the front lawn, perambulator and all, would be much simpler than breaking in. And one of the houses sits at the corner. Quick getaway around the next street and down an alley."

"Yes, I see what you mean. What file are you looking at?"

Hodgins turned one of the sheets around so Barnes could read it.

"Mrs. Brown? I don't understand."

Hodgins leaned back, trying to decide what to say. *It's going to come out, eventually.* "Barnes, shut the door. What I'm about to tell you is to be kept in strict confidence, at least for now."

Barnes sat on the edge of the chair. "You can trust me."

"I know. Do you remember Mrs. Brown's condition when I arrested her?"

"Yes. Didn't she give birth about two months or so later?"

"Correct. The baby, a boy, was put in the Protestant's Orphan Home until they found suitable parents. We place babies much quicker than older children. As I have her two other children, I asked to be secretly informed when their brother was adopted. The lawyer that handles the paperwork for the home is an old classmate from Osgoode Hall." He paused while the constable processed the information.

Barnes' jaw dropped, his eyes wide. "You mean…?"

"Little Alfie Throckmorton. I was hoping to find mention of next-of-kin in Mrs. Brown's file, but only her dead husband is listed. Maybe a brother or another relative found out about the baby and took him back."

"What about Holly and Ivy?"

"What about them?"

"If a relative reclaimed the baby, maybe—"

"He'll try for the twins?" Hodgins finished Barnes' sentence. "Yes, that thought crossed my mind. More than once. It wouldn't be difficult to find out I have them. It's not exactly a secret. But how would they know where the baby went? I need to make two more stops. First to the Orphan Home, secondly the prison."

Hodgins had a nodding acquaintance with the matron at the Home, Mrs. Large. "I need to go over and speak with the matron. She if she's willing to give me any information. Then I'll go to the Don and check if the warden will allow an unscheduled visit with Mrs. Brown. Don't expect me back for a while."

As he made his way to the massive brick building, Hodgins tried to think up some way to find out if someone had tampered with the records, without making it sound like they had been negligent. If someone had broken in and rifled through their files, the matron would never report it. The privacy of the children and the new parents was of the utmost importance. As far as the detective knew, Matron Large didn't even know he'd been kept informed about Alfie.

The detective stood in front of 20 Sullivan Street, relieved Holly and Ivy hadn't stayed in this place long. Only had to stay a few months while all the legalities were dealt with. He walked up the steps and entered. Expecting the sounds of children, it surprised Hodgins to be met with quiet. *Matron must be strict.* Footsteps echoed in the open hallway, getting louder as someone approached.

"May I help you, sir? Are you here for a child?" The young woman's eyes held hope. Even though the task was impossible, the wish was for every child to find a suitable home.

"Already have three." Hodgins smiled. "Two were here briefly. I need to speak to Matron Large. It's quite urgent. Police business."

She glanced at the badge. "Wait here, please." She scurried up a flight of stairs, leaving him in the hall.

Hodgins glanced inside the room to his right. It filled the space between the hallway and the far wall, encompassing the three windows facing the street. A small piano sat quietly in the corner. A sofa had been pushed against the side wall, a small table in front, with a pair of uncomfortable looking wooden chairs opposite. *Wonder what they use this room for? Showing off the children to prospective parents?*

He jumped when the woman silently returned and addressed him. "This way, sir." A faint grin twitched on her lips.

"I'll bet you were a handful as a child." He grinned back. "How'd you manage to return without making a sound?"

Her smile widened. "I really couldn't say. Follow me. Matron doesn't like to be kept waiting." She led him to a small office, closing the door when she left.

Hodgins recalled his earlier visit with the woman running the home when adopting the twins. Her appearance hadn't changed. Her greying hair sat atop her head in a tightly wound bun, wire-rimmed glasses perched on the tip of her nose. *How do they not fall off?*

"Thank you for seeing me, Matron Large. Won't take up much of your time."

"I remember you. There's no problem with the twins, I trust? It's most difficult to find a suitable home for siblings. Especially twins. We don't have them come through our doors often."

"No problems at all. Great addition to our family. I do have a rather delicate question about their brother." He waited, expecting a stern lecture on the privacy of their wards. It didn't come.

Matron stared at Hodgins, lightly tapping her fingers on the desk. She finally spoke. "You know I can't tell you where he is."

"I already know. What I need to find out is whether or not you've had a break in." He held up his hand before she could answer. "Hear me out. As I said, I know the Throckmortons took him in. I was a little wrong saying I know where the baby is. You see, Matron, someone snuck into the house and took him. It looks like the thief went after him specifically. I don't expect any details from you, and I won't report the break in, but I need to know if this is where the thief could have obtained the address."

Matron Large glanced at a file cabinet near her desk. "He's been stolen?"

"Yes. Along with some of his clothing and cloth diapers. Have you any reason to believe anyone has been through your files?"

The detective could tell she struggled with her conscience and duty as she bit her bottom lip and sighed several times. He waited while she made up her mind.

"I don't know how that information would help you locate the child, but yes, I found his file pulled out of the drawer and left on the floor."

"So someone would have the address of the Throckmorton's from the file?"

"Yes, that information is there."

He stood. "Thank you for being honest. That confirms my theory. There were several opportunities to easily take a child from other homes on the street. The culprit took the time to climb a tree for Alfie, rather than grabbing a child left sleeping in a pram on the front lawn. If you ever have any problems in the future, you can trust me to assist, off the record."

"I doubt we'll need your help, but I'll keep your offer in mind. Please, let me know when the child is found."

Hodgins bowed his head. "Of course. I'll see myself out." He left the building and headed to his next stop. The Don Gaol.

CHAPTER FIVE

Hodgins stopped as he approached the building. Looking up, a stone carving of Father Time stared down at him from above the doorway. Inside, numerous wrought-iron serpents and dragons connected the walls to balconies and catwalks. *Probably attempts to scare the inmates.* As his trip was unplanned, he asked to speak directly with the warden. After explaining the reason for his visit, the warden allowed a short interview with Mrs. Brown. Ten minutes later, they sat face to face.

She scowled at Hodgins, sitting with her arms crossed. "Ain't got nothin' more to say to ya. And I ain't got no more children for you ta steal."

"Strange you should put it like that. Do you have any enemies that would have reason to want your children?"

She narrowed her eyes. "Waddaya mean?"

"To put it bluntly, someone has taken your son."

"Taken? Lenny wouldn't..." She shut her mouth, reluctant to say anything further.

"Lenny? Was he part of your husband's gang?"

No answer. She continued to scowl, narrowing her eyes.

"Is Lenny someone who'd harm him? If you have any feelings for your child, please help me find him. Remember, I saw you with the twins before your arrest. You were a caring mother."

Hodgins took in her appearance while waiting for an answer. Despite being in her thirties, she looked closer to fifty. Her stay in prison for the past year had hardened and aged her. The prison clothing hung on her now boney frame. It was difficult for him to picture how she looked when they first met. An extremely attractive and shapely woman, even when round with child.

"Did he go to a good home?"

"Yes. I've met them and they seem quite nice. Their home is lovely and they have a cook and a maid. Alfie even has his own room. Please, who is Lenny?"

"They named him Alfie?" She made a face like she'd just bit into a lemon. "Suppose they had their reasons."

"His father said they named him for Alfred the Great. Now, please, who is Lenny?"

"Cousin of my late husband. Black sheep of the family." She laughed at Hodgins' reaction. "Yes, worse than my husband. If he keeps the boy, when he's older, he'll be little more than a servant, constantly on the run and trained as a thief. Find him."

Hodgins stood to leave, but she stopped him. "Wait. Tell me about the twins. They're well?"

"Yes. Since we didn't know their names, my daughter thought we should call them Holly and Ivy, seeing as it was Christmas. They're happy and living in a house full of love. We only wish we could have taken the baby boy as well."

"Holly and Ivy? Yes, I like those names. I remember how you were with them when we first met. They're with a good family."

The detective rose, bowing slightly to the inmate and tipping his homburg. "I'm so glad I have your approval." He chuckled, shaking his head as he exited.

* * *

As soon as he returned to the station, Hodgins asked Riddell to go through their records, looking for anything on Lenny Brown.

"Since his cousin had already come to Toronto, check to see if there's any record of Lenny arriving in the city. I doubt you'll find anything, but you may as well look."

"Brown?" Riddell cocked his head. "Related to Anthony Brown? The one who framed your brother for murder?"

"Actually, it was his wife doing that, but yes, his cousin. Anthony moved with his family to start new, supposedly, but you remember how that turned out? Maybe his cousin followed him."

"I'll see what I can uncover."

"Good. I'll send a telegram to the Boston Police. That's where my brother first got mixed up with that lot."

"Is there something specific I should watch out for?" Riddell started across the room towards the files, aided by a walking stick.

Limp's barely noticeable. Glad he's not being kidded by the other constables. Must hurt like the dickens. "Known associates, last known locations. That sort of thing. Only go back to say, September of '75. He was probably in Boston before that. Don't even know for certain he came up, just a thought." Hodgins pointed at the crutch replacement. "Crutches a little too much?" He smiled as he pictured the tangled mess at the Throckmorton's.

"Since the limp is permanent, I didn't want to wrestle with those things for the rest of my life. Besides, they hurt my armpits. Found this in a pawnshop." Riddell leaned back on a desk and held the walking stick up. "Fancy topper. Must have cost an important person a month's pay."

Hodgins took it for a closer look. Someone had carved the top in the shape of a very detailed lion, with a band of engraved pewter below it. The top of the head was worn smooth from use. "Someone's fall from status is your good fortune. Looks well-made, and can double as a weapon." He handed it back. "I'd better get that telegram sent and arrange for my trip down to Boston."

An hour later, Harrington knocked on the detective's door. Hodgins waved him in.

"Sir, I've found stories in the papers about a couple of young ladies who killed themselves using quicksilver. They didn't bother to investigate as they weren't society women."

"You mean they were ladybirds? Probably tired of the lifestyle."

"It just said one had loose habits. The other was a known alcoholic."

"Coincidence. Why don't you stop chasing nothing and assist Barnes in tracking down that other doctor? The landlady said someone else had been sent prior to Doctor Coward."

Harrington's shoulders slumped. "Yes, sir."

"Appreciate your initiative, but I'm sure it's nothing."

As Hodgins prepared to go home, a reply came in from the Boston Police. The telegram said they'd have all the information available when he arrived. He recalled when his brother, Jonathan, came up. He had to change trains during the long trip. This would be a week-long journey there and back, but it would be quicker than waiting for the mail to come up, and he expected an in-person visit would provide more details. He folded the telegram and tucked it in his pocket as he exited the station house.

* * *

Delia wagged a finger in her husband's face when he told her he'd be gone for such a long time. "The twins' party is barely a week away. Don't you dare stay any longer than necessary. It's their first proper party with us and you simply can't miss it."

Hodgins reached out, grabbed her finger, and kissed it. "Five days at most. Promise."

Slightly mollified, her Irish temper softened. "Why can't they just write you a letter?"

"If the Browns are as bad as I believe, the officer tasked with writing it would develop a hand cramp. Little things wouldn't be included, and those little things often turn out to be important. I'll pick up whatever they've prepared, and speak to any officer with knowledge of the family. Then I'll take the first train back. I've reviewed the Grand Trunk schedule and memorized the return times."

He reached into his pocket for his notebook to show Delia his planned schedule. "Train for Montreal leaves at 8:30 tomorrow morning. I'll have to stay overnight. The train to Boston leaves the next morning at 9:30. Will be quite late when I get to Boston. One day there to chat with the local police, then basically the same schedule back, staying overnight in Montreal again. Gives me a full day before the party."

"I'm a little frightened, Bertie. What if the person who took Alfie comes for Holly and Ivy?"

"I'll speak with Barnes and Harrington before I leave. Riddell, too. Have them take turns keeping watch. Maybe Riddell can gather up an armload of old newspapers and look for clues about the unknown doctor who attended Miss Jackson before Doctor Coward became available. Think you can put up with him a few days?"

"Certainly. Tom's a good lad. Be nice to have an adult to talk to while Beryl is busy with the girls. Do you think he's well enough to accompany me when I take the girls for a stroll?"

"As long as you keep it short. He's got a fancy walking stick now, but too long a walk will cause him discomfort. More than I believe he lets on."

Delia clicked her tongue. "Men. Let the least little thing seem like a catastrophe. Probably more self-conscience than anything else. Maybe I should put him in the perambulator." She smiled. "Don't worry. I won't tire him out."

CHAPTER SIX

Hodgins woke early, packed his travel bag, then tiptoed down to the kitchen after lighting a small fire in the bedroom fireplace. He sliced several thick pieces from the leftover ham and wrapped them in a cloth, along with two of the biscuits Delia baked the previous day. A third biscuit smothered in her homemade peach jelly went into his empty belly, along with a cup of hot tea. Before leaving, he stepped over the dog and started a small fire in the potbelly stove. It would be nice and hot when Delia rose. Scraps didn't even open his eyes.

Since he would be leaving in less than an hour, the detective detoured to the police station and left written instructions for the three constables before catching the train. A cabriolet approached, and he flagged it down.

When he arrived at the train station, the platform bustled with people waiting for the train or a passenger. Porters stood by those with numerous trunks, ready to load them when the train arrived.

He chatted briefly with Harold, one of the station agents, while waiting for departure. "Ever been to Boston?"

"Can't say I have. Would be nice to visit, but with the entire family, it's too expensive. Maybe when the children are grown and on their own."

"That's right. You have a large family. Five, is it?"

Harold nodded.

"I've been down only once, for my brother's wedding. It's quite lovely in the spring. Jonathan mentioned the winters can be harsh at times. Says the amount of snow is unbelievable."

When the whistle blew, Hodgins went out to the platform, flipping a coin to the newsboy. Once most of the passengers settled on the train, he got in, found an empty seat, then leaned back with the open newspaper over his face, and snoozed.

* * *

Two days later, dusty and exhausted, Hodgins checked into a hotel recommended by one of the Boston train porters.

The hotel had a restaurant on the main floor, just off the lobby. His room was small, but the bed was soft and unexpectedly comfortable. He woke later than planned, but still had plenty of time for his inquiries, asking at the front desk for directions to police headquarters at 154 Berkeley

Street. After jotting down the instructions, he ordering a large breakfast.

It was well past ten when he finally walked into the police station. Hodgins stopped inside the door, taking a minute to look around. *Lot bigger than ours. Busier, too.* He asked a passing constable where he could find Captain Barrett.

"He's wicked busy. One of the constables will talk to you."

Hodgins had forgotten the peculiar Boston accent and figures of speech. "He's expecting me. Detective Hodgins, Toronto Constabulary."

"That's up there in Canada, right? This way." As he led the visiting detective to Barrett, he asked what Hodgins first thought was a joke. "Got much snow up there?"

Hodgins laughed. The constable stopped and turned, waiting for an answer. *He's serious. I'll play along,* "Seeing as it's May, we've only a foot or so. Should be gone by July." Somehow he managed to keep a straight face.

The constable nodded, continuing down the hall to the next office. "Sir, detective from Toronto for you." He backed out and closed the door.

Barrett held out his hand. "Nice to meet you, Detective Hodgins. I heard a bit of that conversation. Not one of the brightest on the force, but he's good. I'll let him know you were joking, eventually." He pointed at the chair by his desk.

"Have a seat. Now, if memory serves, your brother got into a spot of trouble with the Browns."

"Yes. I'm happy to say Jonathan's learned his lesson and is doing well in Toronto. I'm certain he won't make any more shady deals. I guess you're wondering why the urgent need for more detailed information than would fit in a telegram?"

The Boston captain nodded. "I read the news about Mrs. Brown having her husband and one of his associates killed. Framed your brother in the process."

"Yes. I suppose you know the Browns had twin girls, another on the way?"

The captain's eyebrows shot up. "Had no idea she was expecting. Sent to an orphanage with the twins, I imagine?"

"Actually, my wife and I have the twins. The baby boy found a home not too long after birth. Only in care for a few months. He's the reason for the interest. Someone has taken him. Mrs. Brown mentioned Lenny when I spoke to her."

"Thunderation! Stole the baby?" He stroked his beard. "The Browns are a tight family. Not really surprised to hear they took the boy back. Raise another little thief. Soon as they can walk, they learn 'em to pick pockets. If you're worried about the girls, don't be. It'll be boys they want."

"My wife will be relieved to hear that. I've got my constables watching over the house."

Barrett slid a short stack of papers across his desk. "Prepared a list for you. Members of the family and associates. Including their last known location. Also included a list of what they're capable of, and a brief description of their crimes." He tapped one of the names. "This one is fast with a knife. Never killed anyone we know of, but he's disfigured many men and women. If he gets his hands on that boy…"

Hodgins nodded, understating the unspoken. "Do you have photographs of any of them? Particularly Lenny. Mrs. Brown mentioned him specifically."

The captain stood. "Should be something in the files. Don't know why I didn't think of that. You won't have any idea what that lot looks like." He stepped out of his office and gave instructions to the closest constable. Photographs of each family member were brought in quickly. "We have several copies. You can take these with you."

Hodgins examined the pictures and tried to recall if he'd seen any of them. None looked familiar. "I'll have one of my constables duplicate these to show around the city. He's quite good with the new equipment we have, and he's training one of our permanently injured constables. It will be quite useful to have our own police photographer. Cheaper than hiring one, and we get the results faster."

Barrett nodded. "City's always on us about our budget. We managed to get our own equipment last year."

Hodgins spent most of the day with members of the Boston Police, chatting with some of the officers who had first-hand experiences with the Brown family. He had almost a dozen pages of his notebook filled with tidbits on their habits, and which ones were skilled with which weapons. Fortunately, the one handy with a knife, The Butcher, was currently in jail.

Hodgins shook the captain's hand. "It's been a long, full day. Thank you for filling me in on the Brown family. Lenny is currently the only real suspect we have, and I don't even know if he's in Toronto."

"Glad to help. I hope you find the child alive and well."

Hodgins decided to treat himself to a good seafood meal rather than eating at his hotel again, going to one of the more popular restaurants, The Union Oyster House. As the waiter placed the plate of fresh oysters before him, Hodgins licked his lips.

When the waiter cleared the table, Hodgins asked him to give his compliments to the chef. "Beats the food the railway serves on the train. Tastiest thing I've had for days.

The memory of fresh-from-the-bay oysters will last until I get home."

The waiter looked down his nose. "I shan't tell the chef you compared his cooking to railway food, but I'll pass along the compliment."

* * *

After breakfast at the hotel, Hodgins requested a few sandwiches for the long ride home, putting off eating the stale train fare as long as possible.

By the time the last leg of his journey ended, most of the city slept. Hodgins began the walk home in the dark, hoping to spot a cabriolet along the way. A few blocks from the station, a carriage pulled alongside him and stopped.

"Hodgins? That you?" The Chief Inspector leaned out of the door.

"Yes. Just back from Boston. Hope the trip was worth it."

"Hop in. My driver can take you home after he drops us off."

The weary detective climbed into the fancy carriage, startled to see a woman.

"My wife, Henrietta. Dear, this is Detective Hodgins. My best detective. Dare I say the best in the city?"

Hodgins removed his homburg. "Ma'am. Pleased to meet you. Forgive my rumpled appearance. I've had a long journey on the train. You both look dressed for the theatre."

"Yes, we attended the performance of Rob Roy at the Grand Opera House. Highly recommend it." The Chief Inspector proceeded to tell Hodgins all about it and the wonderful acting.

Henrietta nodded. "The Scottish songs were difficult to follow, but their voices were magnificent. I'm glad we managed to get tickets before the show closed. Tonight was the last performance."

Hodgins smiled. "If time permits, maybe I'll purchase tickets for a performance at The Grand soon. My wife enjoys a break from the children from time to time. We haven't been for quite some time."

After leaving the Inspector and his wife at their home and thanking them for the lift, Hodgins gave his address to the driver. Even though the carriage was owned by the inspector and not a hire, Hodgins tossed the driver a coin. "I know you'd like to get to bed as much as me. It's already close to midnight and you've been taken out of your way."

"Thank you, sir." The driver flicked the reins and the horse trotted off.

Hodgins entered his house as quietly as possible, hoping Scraps wouldn't wake and start barking. The dog softly padded down the hall, tail wagging. Too sleepy to jump up, Scraps sat in front of his master.

"Good boy." He knelt and give the dog a long scratch behind the ears. "I'm off to bed. You go back to your rug." As he passed the sitting room, he glanced in at the covered figure snoring on the sofa.

CHAPTER SEVEN

When Hodgins woke, the sun shone through the window. He looked at the clock on the mantle of the small fireplace in the bedroom. His eyes popped open. "Ten thirty! The Inspector will not be pleased."

Dressing quickly, he rushed downstairs. "Why didn't you wake me, Delia?"

"Calm down. Floyd said he'd tell everyone you were checking a few things before you went in. Now sit down. I've fixed you a big breakfast."

Between bites of eggs, sausages, and biscuits, he filled Delia in. Some of the stories he relayed shocked her.

"They sound like a truly horrid family. Do you really believe one of them would have come up for the boy?"

"It's possible. How have things been here? No trouble? My lads keep an eye on everything?"

"They were a great comfort and help. The twins really took to Tom. He kept them amused for hours."

"I hope he found time to do a little police work." Hodgins smiled and took a sip of tea.

"He made excellent use of our dining table. I've never seen so many newspapers. Tom must have found something useful, as he frequently made notes."

"Is that who I heard snoring when I came in? Did Tom stay all night?"

"No. Floyd sent him home and stayed. Tom arrived about three hours ago, so Floyd went home to change. Tom went to fetch today's early edition of *The Globe* a few minutes ago. Should be returning any time now."

Scraps barked and raced to the front door, tail wagging.

"Must be him now." Cordelia took another teacup from the cupboard.

The door opened and closed.

Delia answered her husband's raised eyebrow. "I told him just to knock and walk in."

A moment later, the constable joined them in the kitchen, the dog leading the way, the end of Riddell's walking stick in his mouth. "Morning, sir. Glad to have you back. Too bad we couldn't work from home all the time. Got so much done." Tom sat, letting Scraps drag the walking stick over to his rug.

"Work from home? Nice idea, but I can't see that ever happening. Delia said you've been making notes from the newspapers."

Riddell smiled at Cordelia when she handed him a fresh cup of tea. "Yes. Still haven't found the doctor that attended Miss Jackson before Doctor Coward, but I noticed several strange things. Harrington mentioned finding a couple of women who died from quicksilver, and I came across even more. Over a half dozen in the past six months."

The detective sat back, thinking. "I know I told him it was nothing, but you two may be on to something. Put your heads together and write up a report. List anything that ties them together. If your reasoning is sound, we'll look into it further. Now, you settle in. I'm going back to the train station with the photographs they gave me in Boston. I'll talk to Harrington about your findings when I go back to Station Four."

They chatted over tea for a quarter of an hour, then the detective made his way down to Union Station to speak with the ticket agent.

"Afternoon, Harold. I have a few photos I'd like you to look at." Hodgins laid the prints out on the ticket booth counter. "Any of these fellows get off a train in the last few weeks?"

"A lot of people go through here, Detective. Anything make these ones stand out?"

"Other than their ugly mugs? Nothing."

Harold looked over each picture. "Can't help. Sorry. Train's pulling out soon. Once the platform's clear, check with the porters. Unfortunately, if it's been weeks, they've likely forgotten."

Since the weather was pleasant, Hodgins sat on a bench outside the ticket booth, people watching. His mind flipped back and forth between the death of Miss Jackson and the abduction of Alfie, barely a year old. *Are Holly and Ivy safe? Was the captain in Boston correct assuming they only wanted the boy? Is it even one of the Browns?*

The whistle blew, signaling the train was preparing to leave, interrupting his thoughts. Most of the people had either boarded or left the station. The porters became available after they took the luggage to the waiting carriages for the arrivals and took care of the ones departing. Hodgins approached the closest one and introduced himself.

"I know I'm probably asking the impossible, but do you recall any of these men arriving in the last ten days?"

The porter sifted through the pictures. "Sorry. Don't look familiar."

One by one, he asked, receiving a negative answer from each porter. As he left the platform, he stopped, smacking his forehead with this hand. "Stupid! They'd likely taken the same route I did. I need to talk to the night porters."

Hodgins went back inside to ask when the porters handling the late trains would be in.

"Only have two on nights, as there aren't many passengers on them. Come back around ten. Won't be a train 'til quarter past, so you'll have time to talk to them."

The detective waved down a passing cabriolet to take him to the police station.

* * *

The detective climbed the steps to the station house, yawning despite the extra sleep. He nodded at the sergeant on the way to his office, barely noticing someone running across the room.

"Welcome back, sir. Was the trip useful?" Barnes followed Hodgins into his office.

"Gathered a lot of information. How relevant it is remains to be seen. We still have no proof it was one of the Browns. They did confirm no one has seen Lenny for several weeks." He handled the photographs to Barnes. "Duplicate these and print up several copies. Show them around. Maybe we'll get lucky and someone will recognize one of them. I'll need these back before I leave. Have to return to Union Station tonight to show them to the night porters."

The senior constable took the prints. "I'll get started right away."

"Send Harrington in on your way. Save me from hollering across the room."

When Harrington arrived, Hodgins waved him to the chair. "Riddell told me he's been uncovering even more quicksilver deaths. Why don't you join him at my house to write up a report? Before you go, have you uncovered anything new regarding Miss Jackson's death?"

Harrington lower himself onto the chair, folding his six-foot, five-inch frame to fit. "Not much to tell. I spoke to her friend, Gertie. I mean Miss Dickson. She did say one thing of interest. You recall that Miss Jackson spent time with a few of the single men from Elliot's?"

Hodgins nodded, taking note of the slight blush when Floyd mentioned Miss Dickson.

"Well, seems one of them was particularly interest in her. Obsessed, she told me. Apparently, Miss Jackson had even taken the train to visit her brother one weekend recently, because he kept coming to the front door."

Hodgins became more interested. "Visited her brother? Funny. He said he hadn't seen her for months. Did she mention the name of the unwanted caller or when exactly she took the train?"

"No." Harrington opened his notebook to the last page of notes. "She was in a hurry. Here it is. Just said *recently*, then she had to rush off to her cousin's as she was already late. Sorry, should have delayed her further."

"Good work. It's not often we have two mysteries to solve at once. Glad you lads are able to use lulls in one to investigate the other. Unfortunately, I've seen my share of coppers sitting on their rumps, waiting for a lead to come to them, ignoring anything else going on. I'll see if I can catch her when she clocks off. Now, go join Riddell. No doubt my wife will find something to feed you."

Harrington stood, grinning. "Maybe she's baked a pie or cake?"

The detective laughed. "With three children in the house, it's not often we don't have something sweet." He waved the constable out the door. *Hmm. A Victoria Sponge would be nice.*

Hodgins suddenly remembered the date and hurried after Harrington. "Don't forget the twins' party tomorrow."

As Saturday was a working day for most of Hodgins' acquaintances, people would be coming in and out all afternoon. When he requested the day off, he made certain to extend an invitation to the Chief Inspector. When the Chief expressed regret he couldn't make it, Hodgins was relieved such a senior person in the force wouldn't be there.

The detective spent the rest of the afternoon reading and re-reading reports for both cases. Barnes returned the pictures of the Browns after photographing them, then distributed his prints among those still in the station.

With no leads in either case to follow, Hodgins went to several boarding houses near the railway. One by one, he showed the pictures to the landlords. No one recognized the faces. Several barely glanced at them. Many of the lower-class boarding houses didn't want any dealings with the police, as the majority of their tenants weren't law-abiding citizens.

The time finally came to catch Miss Dickson on her way home. Hodgins waved down a passing hansom and had the driver wait in front of Elliot's. The young lady walked out the front door five minutes later.

"Miss Dickson? A word, please." Hodgins jumped off and approached her. "I have a couple of questions. A lift? We can talk on the way." He flashed a smile that Cordelia often told him would easily land him in trouble with the wrong lass.

She flirted with the detective, batting her eyelashes. "Why detective, I'd be happy to accept a ride with you."

He helped her up and she settled a little closer to him than proper. *Uh-oh. I'd better watch this one. Harrington can make any further inquiries.*

Hodgins slid a couple of inches away, earning a frown from the young lady. "I'd like to ask you about your conversation with Constable Harrington. You said one of your co-workers was giving Miss Jackson more attention than she wanted. Could you tell me his name?"

"I don't want to get anyone in trouble." Gertie lowered her head slightly, trying to appear coy.

"We simply need to speak with him. It's most urgent."

"Well, I suppose I can tell *you*." She smiled and batted her eyelashes again. "It's not really a secret. Toby. Tobias Hinds, but you just missed him."

Hodgins wrote down his name. "One more thing. Do you recall exactly which weekend Miss Jackson took the train to visit her brother?"

"Oh, yes. Spoiled my weekend. We were supposed to go see *Camille* at the Grand. Three weeks ago."

Hodgins added that to his note. "And she only has the one brother? Samuel, up in King?"

"That's the one. She took the train that Saturday and returned late Sunday."

Hodgins glanced outside. "Looks like we're almost at your boarding house. Do you recall any other gentleman Miss Jackson had trouble with?"

She shook her head. "Only Tobias."

The driver stopped the horse directly in front of the walkway to the front porch.

"One more stop, Stan. Be right back." Hodgins assisted Gertie down and walked her to the front door.

Before entering, Gertie turned, giving him her best demure look. "Would you like to come in for tea?"

"Thank you, but no. My wife will have dinner started." He opened the door and held it for her, then hurried back to the waiting cab.

Stan sat holding the reins, grinning from ear to ear. "That one's likely to end up in trouble if she ain't careful. Heading to the missus now?"

"Fast as you can. My constables can deal with this one from now on. I believe one of them has a soft spot for her." He laughed and climbed in.

Fifteen minutes later, he walked into the kitchen. Cordelia stared at him, wiping her hands on her apron. "Gracious, Bertie. Your face is as red as my strawberry tarts."

He kissed her freckled cheek and stole a freshly baked scone, not waiting for it to cool. "Not used to having young lassies flirt with me. Must be getting old."

She passed him an almost empty jar of her strawberry jam. "You may be twelve years older than when I married you, but you're every bit as handsome. More so, actually. One of the store clerks? The young lady at the book store has a soft spot for you."

"No. Friend and co-worker of the dead woman. If I have any more questions for her, Tom or Floyd can interview her. Henry certainly wouldn't be able to handle her." He looked around. "Where's Scraps? Missed getting bowled over at the door."

"Look out back."

Hodgins peered through the kitchen window. The three girls were outside. Riddell sat on a chair, bouncing one of the twins on his knee. Sara had the other. Harrington played fetch with Scraps.

"Looks like fun. Think I'll join them."

As he headed for the back door, Cordelia called after him. "I've invited them to stay for dinner."

Hodgins and Harrington threw the ball around for Scraps until Delia called them to dinner. After the constables finally went home and the dishes were cleaned and put away, Hodgins settled in front of a low burning fire to read the report that Tom and Floyd prepared. Cordelia joined him after putting the twins to bed.

"You look exhausted, Delia. Why don't you stay in bed an extra hour in the morning? I'll feed the girls."

"There's so much to do for the party. I thought I'd get up early."

Hodgins put the report on his lap. "Nonsense. Didn't you ask Beryl to come over early to help?"

"Well, yes, but—"

"No buts. Can't have you falling asleep in front of our guests. You'll stay in bed and I'll be cook and nanny until she arrives. In fact, why don't you go to bed now?"

Delia smiled weakly. "That's a good idea, unfortunately I don't believe I have the strength to get out of this chair."

"I believe I can help with that." He swept her up in his arms and carried her up the staircase. "You haven't gained an ounce since I first carried you over the threshold." He sat her on the edge of the bed and kissed her forehead. "Now, get some sleep."

CHAPTER EIGHT

As promised, Hodgins let Cordelia sleep in. After dressing, he lit a small fire in the bedroom fireplace to combat the early morning spring chill, then roused Sara.

"Your mother has a busy day, so I'm letting her sleep in. You get the twins dressed and I'll make breakfast. Eggs and sausages suit you?"

"Daddy, that's the only thing you can cook." Sara giggled and got out of bed. "We'll be down by the time you have breakfast ready."

Sara joined in to help with the dishes after everyone finished eating. Scraps padded down the hall and woofed quietly. Hodgins patted his head as he approached, opening the door before Beryl could knock.

"Thank you for coming early and giving up your day off. You'll have time to enjoy the party once it starts. Delia's parents will keep an eye on the children while we attend to the guests. I've let her have a lie in." He took her cape and hung it on the coat tree.

"When did she find time to do all this?" Beryl looked around at the pink and white bunting wrapped around the upstairs railing. More hung on the walls of the sitting and dining rooms.

"I put that up last evening after sending her to bed. She practically fell asleep in the chair. Still have the backyard to decorate. Henry's coming over with tables and chairs soon. John Mitchell is loaning him a wagon from his livery. I just had to promise him a large piece of cake."

The mantle clock chimed. "Better get her up. Said I'd let her sleep an extra hour, and it's been over ninety minutes. If you wouldn't mind fixing breakfast for her, I'll wake her. Sausages are cooked. Just need warming.

"Of course. Sara can keep an eye on Holy and Ivy." She looked around. "Where are they?"

"Sara's finishing up in the kitchen, and the twins are with her." He glanced down the hall. "They are awfully quiet."

They hurried to the kitchen. Sara was wiping off the table and the twins sat in their chairs, half asleep. Sara look up when they entered.

"Morning, Beryl. It's going to be such a fun day. Daddy, shouldn't Mommy be up soon?"

"Just about to do that, Pumpkin. I think these two monkeys need to go back to bed, though."

Holly raised her arms when she spotted him. "I'll take this one. You grab Ivy. Beryl will start Mommy's breakfast." He grinned when the nanny's tummy growled. "Maybe she'll join Mommy for breakfast."

Beryl blushed. "I did leave the house rather early."

Sara put two plates on the table before lifting Ivy from her chair and taking her upstairs. "You did a good job decorating, Daddy. Mommy will be pleased."

"Still have a lot more to do." He laid Holly on her bed. "No point changing them. They'll be in their party dresses soon enough."

He crossed the hall to rouse his wife and stood beside the bed, staring at her. She stirred, half opening her eyes.

"Why are you staring at me? I must look a fright." Cordelia swung her legs to the side of the bed, sitting up.

"You never look a fright. You looked so peaceful I hated to wake you." He cupped her chin with his hand, tilted her head, then kissed her.

She smiled. "What a wonderful way to wake up." She noticed the hint of sunlight coming through the window. "What time is it?"

"Just gone seven-thirty. And before you say anything, everyone's fed and Beryl is here. She's making your breakfast."

Hodgins stayed with Delia while she dressed and fussed with her hair, updating her on the progress of the morning. "Henry should be here shortly with the extra tables and chairs. We'll put those out back, then decorate the yard. Looks like we'll have a beautiful day."

Delia gasped as they ascended the stairs and the bunting came into view. "You did all this and fed the girls? You're amazing, Bertie."

"Yes, I am quite the catch." They both laughed as they made their way to the kitchen.

Delia noticed the extra plate on the table. "I see I won't be eating alone."

"You've worked our poor nanny so hard she hasn't had time to eat." Hodgins winked at Beryl. "Take your time. We've got everything under control."

"I'm starting the cakes, Mommy. You can decorate them when they've cooled."

"Thank you, Sara." Delia turned to Beryl. "Is there anything I can do?"

"Sit and enjoy your breakfast." The nanny dished out their meal while Hodgins answered the knock at the front door. Scraps beat him to it. Henry Barnes stood ready for the leaping dog when the door opened.

"Does he ever run out of energy?" Henry scratched the dog behind his ears, then pushed him off. "Where do you want all that?" He pointed at the wagon sitting out front.

Hodgins followed Barnes' outstretched arm. Three tables and too many chairs to count were tied securely to the wagon. The horse had already begun to doze. "I'll open the side gate, then we can take everything through."

Scraps ran over to investigate the sleepy draft horse, sniffing at its hairy feet. The horse swung its head, and the dog raced into the backyard.

Once the men set up everything, they came back inside for a cup of tea and a scone before Henry returned the horse and wagon.

Delia took a bundle from the ice box. "Henry, give this to Mr. Mitchell. An iced cake won't survive the trip, so I made a spice cake for him. I hope he enjoys it. And make certain you tell him how grateful we are for the loan of his wagon."

Barnes sniffed the cloth-wrapped cake. "Smells heavenly. I'm certain he'll enjoy it. Won't guarantee any of it makes it home to his family." He took another whiff and smiled.

* * *

All afternoon friends, neighbours, and Hodgins' co-workers filtered through the house. When the party finally ended, the three constables the detective worked with most often stayed behind, along with Doctor Stonehouse and Amelia Alarie, Delia's psychic friend. They couldn't resist the opportunity to discuss their two cases. Hodgins' brother, Jonathan, took his family home, as neither he nor his wife enjoyed talking about the cases. He dropped off Cordelia's parents on the way.

Amelia and Henry's wife, Violet, puttered in the kitchen with Cordelia and Sara while the men gathered in the sitting room to talk business.

The doctor started. "Amelia said she's had another vision about the child. Do you know who it is?"

"Yes. We've been keeping it quiet at the request of the family, but it's bound to get out soon with all the questions we've been asking. Henry already knows. What I'm about to tell you doesn't leave this room." He looked at each one, receiving a nod as confirmation.

"You'll all recall the Brown case last year? Holly and Ivy's mother?"

Hodgins received a round of yeses. "Mrs. Brown was with child at the time of her arrest. The baby, a boy, was taken into care and adopted by a couple soon after."

Stonehouse snapped his fingers. "That's why her visions included you. Someone took the twins' brother.

"Correct. Now, I don't entirely believe in Amelia's psychic abilities, but has she seen anything that might help us?"

"Why not ask her yourself while she's here?"

Barnes spoke up. "She did help with the murdered family, sir."

Stonehouse rose. "I'll fetch her right now."

He returned a few minutes later. "She's requested that everyone gather around the dining room table."

Hodgins shrugged. "Why not?"

Cordelia placed the silver candlesticks on the table as the gentlemen moved to the room across the hall.

"Where's Violet?" Barnes looked around.

"She decided to stay in the kitchen." Cordelia grinned. "Finds this all rather frightening."

"Oh, for goodness' sake. I know she's afraid of séances, but we're not trying to talk to the dead tonight." Henry went to have a word with her, but returned alone.

Everyone sat around the table, waiting. Even Sara joined them, as she found it all quite fascinating. She reached for the matches. "May I light the candles?"

Her mother nodded.

Amelia began preparing herself. She closed her eyes and whispered something in her native French. "I am ready.

This would be easier if I had an object belonging to *l'enfant*." Amelia looked at Hodgins. "Have you anything?"

"Only his sisters."

"I can fetch them, Daddy."

The detective looked at his wife. "What do you think?"

"Bring them both. Double the chances. They'll likely sleep through it all, anyway."

Hodgins followed Sara upstairs, each returning with a slumbering child. Sara sat on one side of Amelia, her father on the other. The psychic placed a hand on each child's head.

"I require complete silence, *s'il vous plaît*." She closed her eyes and swayed from side to side, again speaking French.

The candles flickered.

"I sense he is with family. He is unharmed." Again she mumbled in French, then opened her eyes. "That is all. Where he is, I can not tell. *Je regrette*. I am sorry."

"You said family. We suspect a relative, but have no proof. None of the porters at the train station remember seeing any of them." Hodgins stood and handed Ivy to Delia. "Maybe it's a family member the Boston police don't have a photograph of."

"Maybe they hopped the train without a ticket." Riddell half shrugged. "Just a thought."

Hodgins clapped him on the back. "And a good one. What better way for a criminal to move around than hidden in a rail car?"

Eventually, the two junior constables thanked their hosts and left together, sharing the cost of a hansom cab. Cordelia gave them each a piece of cake to take with them. Henry and Violet left shortly after to visit next door with Violet's parents, who missed the party due to a mild illness. As they had plenty of leftover cake, Cordelia sent them off with a chunk large enough to last a couple of days.

"Well, Doctor, it's just you and me left. Glass of whisky?" Hodgins gestured to the room across the hall. "Maybe the women would like a sherry?"

"Not tonight, Albert. Already have plans." The doctor glanced at Amelia.

"And I don't need three guesses to figure out who with." Cordelia turned to Amelia for confirmation.

"*Oui*. Valentine is taking me to Hamlet at Mrs. Morrison's Grand Opera House." She pronounced it *Valenteen*. She kissed Cordelia on the cheek. "*Merci, mon amie*. We will speak again soon."

Hodgins and Cordelia waved them goodnight as the doctor's buggy started down the street, hooves echoing in the early evening silence.

"I believe the doctor is more than a little smitten with your friend, Delia."

She agreed. "I'm certain Amelia is hiding something. Do you think Doctor Stonehouse is planning to propose?"

"I'm sure I don't know. I do know he's not been around as much as usual. If they are planning something, they'll tell us when they're ready."

CHAPTER NINE

Monday morning Barnes rushed into Hodgins' office, excited about something. "Sir, you won't believe it." The constable leaned against the doorframe, taking a few deep breaths.

"Sit down, Henry, and catch your breath. You almost knocked the sergeant over."

Barnes sat slumped on the edge of the chair, elbows resting on his legs. "I'll apologize in a minute. You just won't believe it."

"Yes, you said. I might believe it better if you told me what it is." Hodgins leaned back, waiting for Barnes to calm himself.

"As I made my way in, someone called to me. I recognized right away it was Stan. You know him. Has a big white mare with a black star on her forehead. Well, I don't know how he knows we're looking for Lenny Brown, but he says he saw him after his last fare yesterday."

Hodgins nodded. "I took a cabriolet to go see Miss Dickson after taking the pictures around to some boarding houses. It was Stan's cab. I showed him and asked him to keep an eye out. Where did you see him?"

"Down by the Post Office on Adelaide Street. He'd just dropped off a fare."

"Take Harrington and one of your reproduction photographs. Scour the area. Someone will know where he is." Hodgins stood at the same time as Barnes. "Hold up." He reached into his pocket and drew out some coins. "For the street urchins. They notice quite a bits. See if you can find Backstreet Billy. I haven't heard from him for some time. Hopefully, he's not still working as a runner for the gambling dens."

"I can't take your money, sir."

"Take it. They'll be glad for a coin. I have to make another trip to King to find out why Miss Jackson's brother lied to me."

"But…"

"That's an order, constable."

* * *

Three hours later, Hodgins left the train station in the Village of King and stormed through the rural community to the Jackson farm. Miss Sawyer's gig sat out front again, along with a buggy. *He's got company other than his fiancée. Don't care.* Hodgins banged on the door with his fist, anger building. Jackson answered this time.

The detective didn't wait for Samuel to say anything. "I want to know why you lied to me."

Samuel blinked several times, then stepped out. "Please, detective, lower your voice. The paster is here discussing the wedding, along with Claire's mother. What do you mean? Lied about what?"

"I don't care if the King of England is inside. I demand the truth this time. You told me you hadn't seen your sister for months, but I've just found out she came up three weeks ago, fleeing unwanted attention from a suitor."

Samuel perched on the edge of a wicker porch chair. "It's all rather embarrassing. Yes, she came up. Unfortunately, that Tobias fellow found out and took the next train. The discussion got heated, and I punched him."

"And two weeks later, she's dead. Did it not occur to you the two things were connected?"

They hadn't noticed Miss Sawyer had come to the door. She gasped. "You believe Tobias killed Annabel? But he was in love with her."

"He may have thought if he couldn't have her, no one could. Or maybe you were tired of your sister's loose ways, paid her a visit, slipping quicksilver into her medicine?"

Samuel stood, face red with anger, arms at his side, fists clenched. "Now look here. My sister was not a loose woman. I won't have you spreading such vicious lies. I'd never harm her. She was happy, and I was glad."

Hodgins spread his hands. "I apologize. My intent was to anger you, hoping you'd slip up and admit to something. Are you certain there isn't anything else? Another jealous suitor?" He looked from Sam to Claire.

"No one else that we know of. I'd like to arrange her funeral. Let her rest, finally." Sam sighed, wiping a tear from the corner of his eye. "When can we bury her?"

"Doctor Stonehouse will release her body tomorrow, I believe."

"I'll come down on the morning train. We buried our parents at Saint James Cemetery. Belle will be buried there too."

* * *

By the time Hodgins returned to Toronto, it was late afternoon. The last of his anger dissipated while sitting at the station in King, waiting for the 1:50 train. Before going to the station house, he went to Elliot's to speak with Tobias Hinds.

"Sorry, sir. He didn't show up for work today." One clerk shrugged. "Not certain why."

"I'll need his address."

"He's not there. Mr. Elliot sent me to find him. His mother said he left for work as usual, but he never arrived."

Hodgins sighed. "It's a place to start. Address?"

The detective took the trolley and exited a block from the Hinds' residence. His mind had wondered, trying to figure out where the young lad might have gone, and he nearly missed his stop.

When Hodgins arrived, Mrs. Hinds' eyes were red from crying. When he showed his badge, she stepped out onto the front porch. "Have you found my boy? Has something happened to him?"

"No ma'am. Are you certain he was going to work when he left?"

She stared at the detective. "What do you mean? Where else would he go?"

"He's a young lad. Is it possible Tobias just decided to play hooky?"

"No, never. Something's happened to him. A mother knows." She sobbed as a man came running up the walk. A girl wearing a maid's cap followed. Both panted, trying to catch their breath.

"What's happened? Maid said to come home quick." He wiped the sweat from his brow.

"Toby's gone!" Her sobs turned to wails, so the maid escorted her back inside.

"I'm Detective Hodgins." He showed his badge to Mr. Hinds. "Your son didn't show up for work today. Do you know where he might have gone?"

"Probably with some tart. So, there's no emergency?"

"Not yet."

"Let me know when there is." Mr. Hinds turned and headed back to work, shaking his head.

Hodgins spun around when the back door opened, surprised to see the maid. "You'll have to come another time. The missus is too upset." She closed the door before he could respond.

Maybe the father knows something he didn't want to mention in front of his wife. He ran after Tobias' father. "Mr. Hinds. Wait up."

Tobias' father stopped and turned. "Make it quick. My boss wasn't happy I got pulled away."

Hodgins quickly took in Hinds' attire. Plain trousers, well-worn but not filthy, with a tattered vest over a simple shirt. *Not a business man. Not wearing a suit and tie. And the neighbourhood is quite different from the upper-class area where the Throckmorton's live. Labourer.*

"We can talk while we ride." He flagged down a passing carriage, larger than required, but he recognized the driver.

"Where to, Detective?"

Hodgins turned to Hinds. "Sir?"

Hinds looked at the carriage and the two white horses fastened to it. "Bit much for a trip to the docks."

"My treat. To the docks, Pat."

Once they settled, Hodgins started his inquiries. "Your wife was adamant Tobias met with some sort of mishap, not a rendezvous with a companion. You seem equally certain of the opposite. Has your son made a habit of missing work for such a liaison?"

Hinds had the decency to look ashamed, pulling at this shirt collar. "Well, no. I was just angry at being pulled from work. I'll be docked for certain."

"Would it help if I had a word with your boss?"

"Good Lord, no! That would make it worse. As would this carriage. Drop me off at Clarence Square so no one sees."

Hodgins relayed the location to Pat, then continued with his questions. "His co-workers said your son wasn't one to miss work with no explanation. Are you not concerned that his whereabouts are unknown?"

"Now, see here. I love my son. He's only been missing a few hours. Would you be concerned if your lad of twenty-five was late for work?"

Hodgins chuckled. "No, not overly concerned. However, it is out of character and one of his co-workers has recently been found dead, under somewhat puzzling circumstances."

The carriage came to a halt at their destination, but Hinds make no move to exit. "You mean the Jackson girl? I thought she died from an illness."

"It's true she'd been ill, but there was a poison in her that can't be accounted for."

"Toby has been quite upset over her death. I believe he planned on proposing."

And the answer would have been no. "Can you think of any place he might be? Friends?"

"Not at the moment. If I think of anything, where can I find you?"

"Station House Four, on Wilton Avenue, east of Parliament. Ask for Detection Hodgins. If I'm not there, leave word with the sergeant or one of the constables."

Hinds opened the carriage door. "Too bad I couldn't travel like this all the time. Thank you, detective. Please find my boy." Hinds jumped down and ran the rest of the way to work.

"Where to now, Bert?"

"Back to the station, Pat. Take the long way. Need to think."

Pat walked the horses up Yonge Street, turning west on Queen, away from the station house. He turned again at

Osgoode Hall, heading north to Bloor, then travelled east, giving the detective plenty of time to think. After thirty minutes, Hodgins called out to the driver.

"Stop at Mitchell's Livery. I'll pay John for a bit of feed for Daisy and Buttercup, then walk the rest of the way."

* * *

When Hodgins walked into the station, the three constables sat huddled at Barnes' desk. He joined them. "Found something interesting, lads?"

"We found the boarding house where Brown is staying, but he wasn't there." Riddell looked disappointed and nudged Barnes. "Ask him."

"Ask me what? Henry?"

"Well, we know this case about the stolen baby is rather sensitive, but don't you think it's time we put something in the newspaper? Brown's picture maybe? Don't need to say why we're looking for him."

The detective nodded. "I was having the same thought. Once we let any information out, the rest of the story will soon follow. I'd better prepare the Throckmorton's. I'll do that on my way home. One of you write up something just asking for information on his whereabouts. Leave it on my desk and I'll review it in the morning." He checked his pocket watch. "Should be able to catch the Throckmorton's before their meal."

Twenty-seven minutes later, Hodgins hopped off the trolley and hurried to the Throckmorton's home. When the maid opened the door, the aroma of fresh bread surrounded him. "Evening, Alice. I need a word with the family. Are they in?"

"Yes, sir. Step inside."

Alice scurried upstairs, returning a few minutes later. "They'll be right down. Said you're to wait in here." She indicated the room to the left, where he'd last spoken with them. "Have you found the bloke what took little Alfie?"

"Soon."

When she realized he wasn't going to tell her anything further, she went back to her duties.

Otis Throckmorton came in a few minutes later. "Cassandra is still dressing for our evening meal. Good news, I hope?"

"Yes and no. We believe we know who's behind it, but we haven't located him yet. That's what I need to tell you. In order to locate him quickly, we're going to put his photograph in the newspaper. No details of the child will be included, but it's bound to come out. Reporters always find out information we'd rather they didn't print. I need to prepare you for what they'll uncover. I'd like to have your wife included, as what I need to tell you is rather delicate, and I believe will come as a shock if she hears about it later."

"Now you've got me worried, detective. Maybe you should tell me first?"

"I'd prefer to tell you together. I can answer any questions you have afterwards."

Mrs. Throckmorton entered the room before her husband could object further. She still appeared ill from worry and lack of sleep.

Hodgins stood until she sat. "As I told your husband, I have information about Alfie that you may find disturbing. About his background."

"I don't understand. He's an orphan. Only a tiny baby when we took him in. What sort of background could a baby have?" Otis held his wife's hand.

"The child is not exactly an orphan. His father is dead, but not his mother. Not yet, anyway. There's no easy way to put this, so I'll be blunt. His father was a criminal and his mother is in prison for arranging his murder. He has two older sisters, twins, that my wife and I took in. We need to publish our suspects' likeness in the newspaper and ask the public for information. It won't be long before the reporters discover why we're looking for the man, and who the child is."

The Throckmorton's sat in stunned silence. A gasp sounded from the hall. They all turned and saw the maid at the doorway.

"Cook asks how long to hold supper."

"We'll be there shortly." Otis looked at Hodgins. "Is there anything else?"

Surprised at their lack of response, the detective stammered. "Um… well… no. I expected you to have questions."

"My wife and I will discuss this. It's quite a shock to find out the child was born of criminals." He stood. "Alice will see you out."

They left him alone in the sitting room, more than a little stunned.

The maid appeared again. "It is true? The child has bad blood?"

Hodgins walked to the front door. "His blood is the same as yours or mine. It's not his fault who bore him. Please do not speak about this."

All the way home, Hodgins thought about the reaction to his news. *Peculiar. No questions. No comments. Suppose it was quite a shock.*

He relayed the information to his wife when he arrived home. "I have a bad feeling about this, Delia."

"The maid may have spoken what was on the minds of her employers. Many people believe criminals have some sort of disorder or disease they pass on to their children. Do the Throckmortons strike you as that sort?"

Hodgins thought about his previous discussions with them. "I'm certain his sister does, and she seems to have some influence with him. She's very strong-willed."

"Don't worry yourself over it. Remember how my mother reacted when we first took in the girls? After spending only a few hours with them, they won her over. The Throckmortons have had the boy for almost a year. I'm certain they won't give it a moment's thought. Now, supper's almost ready. Call the girls in and get them washed up."

CHAPTER TEN

The mid-day edition of the local paper, *The Globe*, contained the write-up Hodgins had approved earlier in the morning and personally taken to the newspaper office. He even had the information sent to the *Montreal Evening Star* as the train from Boston routed through there. Shortly after the hawkers had the newspapers, a few people came forward with information. Hodgins sent constables out to investigate each tip. Either the sightings were incorrect or Lenny Brown had left the area. With his likeness in the paper, he'd no doubt lie low.

Barnes had followed up on the most recent sighting, returning to the station just after two. He knocked on the door frame to Hodgins' office and walked in.

The detective looked up from his notes. "From the look on your face, you found nothing, I'm guessing?"

Barnes released a long and heavy sigh. "Nothing. I took the photographs with me, but no one remembers seeing him or any of his family. Not sure I believe them all, but I walked for blocks and came up empty."

"Early days yet. If it was one of the Browns, they won't mistreat him. I've been going through the information from Boston. Lenny has a wife. It's possible she came up with him to care for the child. We've had the trains watched from the start, so I don't think he's gone back down. Boston said they'd keep an eye out in case he slips through our fingers."

Barnes nodded. "It's possible they've headed out of town, somewhere we haven't thought of. Easy enough to hire or purchase a buggy and horse. Could've set up camp deep in the woods until enough time has passed. After a month or so, we'll have fewer men looking."

"I'm not giving up yet." Hodgins pointed at the photographs in Barnes' hand. "Take those and go around to the liveries. See if one of them hired something. I still need to find Tobias Hinds."

The detective went with Barnes to Mitchell's Livery to hire a gig and pony to take him to Elliot's. Gertie Dickson came over as soon as he walked in.

"Have you found Toby yet?" She bit her lip, anxious for news.

"No. Do any of you have any suggestions where he might be?" Hodgins looked around. All the gentlemen clerks except one were busy with customers.

The only employee free leaned on the counter, grinning. "Probably hiding from you, Gert." He looked at Hodgins.

"She's sweet on him and has been trying to land him for almost a year. She's about the only woman around he hasn't stepped out with. Let's see, before Annabel, it was Emma. Or was it Alice? Hard to keep track."

Gertie's eyes narrowed. "Don't talk about him like that. You make his sound like a cad."

Customers stared as her voice raised. Embarrassed, Gertie went back behind the counter, glaring at her co-worker.

Hodgins joined him at the counter, lowering his voice. "Has Mr. Hinds had trouble with women, Mr. Humphries?"

"Yes. He becomes a nuisance. It starts out well enough, then he tries to take up all their free time. Follows them when they go out. Even proposes after only a few weeks. I think he frightens them."

Hodgins nodded towards Gertie, now serving a customer. "He never asked Miss Dickson out?"

"No. She flirts something fierce with him, but he isn't interested." Humphries sighed. "She just doesn't get the hint. Sad, really."

The detective recalled her behaviour when he gave her a lift. "Most men don't like such forward women."

"Exactly. If I were still single, I'd avoid her myself."

"Are you certain you have no idea where he might be? Friends, maybe?"

"Sorry. He's never mentioned friends. I don't think he has any."

"If you think of anything, or he finally shows up, send word to the station."

When Hodgins returned to Station Four, Otis Throckmorton waited in the entry. He stood as soon as he saw Hodgins.

"A quick word, please?" Otis appeared nervous. Uncertain what to do with his hands, he fiddled with his felt Derby hat, crushing the rim.

"My office. We can speak in private." Hodgins led the way.

Otis followed him, closing the door behind him. "I'll get straight to the point. My wife and I discussed this last evening and again this morning. When you find the child, we don't want him back."

Hodgins stumbled, kicking his chair, almost tipping it over. "What do you mean, you don't want him back? Why?"

"If we knew in advance he was damaged, we'd never have taken him. A criminal father and murderess mother. My word! He may grow up to murder us as we sleep."

"Surely you can't believe that? He'll grow up to be the type of person you raise him to be."

Otis opened the office door. "No. We won't take that chance. When you find him, take him back to the home. Good day."

Hodgins followed, watching as Throckmorton exited the station. The detective was still in shock when he returned home that evening.

"Damaged? He actually said that?" Delia dropped onto the chair in the sitting room, landing hard. "But he's still a baby. Maybe once you find him, they'll change their minds. Maybe we could—"

He cut his wife off. "No. We've discussed this. It's too much for you, and we simply don't have the room. Sara would have to double up with the twins."

Cordelia smiled. "We could move to a larger house."

He laughed. "We've barely finished settling in here. Besides, while a larger house would give us more room, it would also mean more cleaning and even more work for you. You know I'm right."

"Yes, but I thought I'd mention it again. Why don't we wait until he's returned before we worry?"

* * *

When Hodgins arrived at his desk the next morning, he found a note from Barnes. Lenny had purchased a wagon and horse from Dominion Livery at 40 King West. Ten minutes later, the constable came in.

"Barnes." Hodgins stood in his office doorway and waved him over. "Got your note. Tell me more."

"It was a day or two after Alfie was stolen. Lenny came in and said he wanted to buy a wagon and horse. Coincidentally, the livery is owned by a Mr. Charles Brown, but he said Lenny is not a relative as far as he knows. Charles tried to rent it to him instead, as he only had the one wagon. Lenny offered him six hundred dollars. Imagine!"

"Quite the incentive. If they're staying awhile, they'll need supplies. Can't be too far from the city. Maybe in one of the villages nearby. Must be a few abandoned farms or shacks. Doubt they'd rent a room at a boarding house. Too easy to find them. I'm certain he brought his wife with him. Get a horse and ride around. Someone must have noticed a couple with a young one in tow."

"Right away, sir."

When Barnes left, Hodgins picked up the report written by Harrington and Riddell. "Let's see what they found out."

He read the two pages, scratching his head. Something in there niggled at his brain, but he couldn't put his finger on it. Hodgins went over to Riddell's desk.

"Very thorough, Tom. Doesn't look like you missed anything."

"You don't look too happy with it, pardon me for saying, sir."

"The report is fine. Excellent, in fact. There's something about it I just can't put my finger on."

"Something I missed?"

"No. A connection I'm not making yet." He leaned against the next desk and re-read it. "The dead ladies. I just can't…" The detective snapped his fingers.

Riddell sat up straight. "You've remembered something. What is it?"

Hodgins sat the papers on the desk, jabbing at the names. "When I was at Elliot's yesterday to see if Tobias Hinds had returned, one of the clerks mentioned some of the beaus Tobias had. He named two. Emma and Alice. Two of the dead ladies in your report are named Emma and Alice. Coincidence? Probably, but I'm going to have a chat with Mrs. Hinds. She should be calmer by now. If anything comes up, I'll be at home afterwards."

Rather than waiting for the horse-drawn trolley or grabbing a passing hansom, Hodgins walked briskly, almost running to the Hinds' residence. He needed time to think about Emma and Alice. *Could they be the same women Tobias fancied? Both dead, just like Annabel. Would Mrs. Hinds be able to fill in the last names of former sweethearts, or should I speak to the husband?*

The detective hesitated before knocking, trying to form his questions so he wouldn't sound accusatory. Seconds after knocking, the front door opened.

"Afternoon. I'd like to speak with your mistress."

The maid opened the door wide and waved him in. "I'll fetch her. Wait in the sitting room." She scampered up the stairs to the second story.

Hodgins used the time to have a good look around. The room appeared much like any other working-class room. As in most homes, a painting of King William IV hung on the wall, much smaller than the one at the boarding house. Old, but well-made furniture, crocheted antimacassars on the backs and arms of the chairs and sofa. A small upright piano sat against the wall, a solitary candelabra sat centred on top. *How could they afford a piano?* None of the candles appeared to have ever been lit. He turned when someone cleared their throat.

"Mrs. Hinds. Thought I'd stop in and check if your son has returned."

She remained by the doorway, hinting the visit would be short. "No. He's still missing. Why haven't you found him?"

He tried to read her tone. *Not upset and not angry. Annoyed?* "I understand he's had a few sweethearts in the past. Could I trouble you for their names? Maybe he's been in touch with one of them or they know where he might be."

A look of disgust crossed her face. "Sweethearts? I believe the correct word would be tart. You've likely had them in your jail a time or two."

"I can check, but I need their full names." *Is she being overprotective? No one good enough for her son?* "Did he tell you their names?"

"Of course. Tobias tells me everything. Alice Marshall was before Annabel. She was lovely. Annabel, that is. Before that, let me think. Emma… Emma Stokes. Maybe it was Ellen Davies. He didn't see those two very long."

Hodgins jotted the names in his little notebook. "Thank you. This information is very helpful. I'm certain we'll locate your son soon."

Mrs. Hinds stepped back into the hall and opened the front door. "I certainly hope so. Good day, detective."

* * *

When Hodgins arrived home, he put the leash on Scraps and took him for a walk. The journey was slow, as the dog had to stop and sniff every few feet.

"So, what do you think, boy? Is young Tobias hiding out of guilt or grief?"

Scraps stopped sniffing and looked at his master. "Woof."

"I don't know either, but I'll figure it out."

They walked to the Ketchum School and Hodgins let the dog run free to play with some local children. They returned home almost an hour later. Scraps trotted to the kitchen, lapped up some water, then fell asleep on his rug.

Cordelia watched as her husband entered the kitchen and sat down with a groan. "Hard day, Bertie?" She poured a cup of tea and placed it in front of him.

"Very. Two troublesome cases with little progress. At least we've had a lead on Alfie. Seems certain Lenny Brown took him, and we assume he's with his wife."

Delia poured another tea and joined him. "That makes sense. If you're going to take a child that young, you'd need a woman to take care of him."

Hodgins blew on his tea, nodding. "Yes, I agree. Also, it would look odd for a man to be travelling alone with the youngster. He'd attract too much attention from ladies asking if he could manage."

Cordelia giggled. "You know how helpless most men are with babies."

"Yes, if they're not used to them. Anyway, he's purchased a wagon and horse, so I guess he's going to lie low for a while. Too far to ride to Boston in a wagon with a stolen infant."

Cordelia rose to remove the potatoes from the heat before the water boiled over. "He'll be hard to find if he's left town."

"Told Barnes to get a horse and ride around. That should keep him busy for several days. Hopefully, he returns with results."

* * *

The first thing Hodgins did upon arriving at work the next morning was find the report Riddell and Harrington had written up. It didn't take long to locate it and the names of the dead women he'd jotted down. Two of them matched the names Mrs. Hinds gave him. Tobias had been involved with two ladies who died unexpectedly. Three, including Annabel Jackson. He waited impatiently in his office for Riddell to come in, pacing circles in front of his desk, periodically going outside to see if he was on his way. The constable finally arrived.

"Tom, where are the newspaper articles you found for Misses Davies and Stokes?"

"In my desk drawer." Riddell moved as fast as he could and opened the top drawer. He reached in and pulled out two newspapers, folded open to the write-ups. "Have you discovered something?"

"Possibly." Hodgins skimmed both stories. Neither had been given much space in the paper. "Both died from quicksilver, just like Miss Jackson. Ruled as overdoses by their own hand."

"Have you discovered something?"

"They all knew Tobias Hinds, and he's not been seen for days. I don't like coincidences."

"You think he killed them? I thought we had accounted for all the quicksilver at the pharmacy."

"We did, but Elliot's isn't the only pharmacy. For now, it's just a line of inquiry. We need to locate Hinds. Barnes will be busy riding from town to town looking for Lenny Brown. I'll take Harrington and scour the city for Tobias. You need to find out what happened to these women."

Riddell nodded. "I'll fetch more back issues from the newspaper. Did you know they call their back files the morgue?"

"Yes, I know. Now go."

"Shall I continue to work at your home?"

The detective thought it over. "No. I don't believe he has any interest in the girls. Stay at *The Globe*. Maybe one of the staff remembers something."

Harrington walked over. "Did I hear you mention my name, sir?"

"Yes. Hope your shoe leather is in good shape."

On the way out, Hodgins explained everything. "May as well start by talking to the dollybirds. See if Hinds has been hanging around. You check the taverns and areas around the docks. I'll inquire along King Street. We can work our way out. Except for Miss Jackson, those types of ladies seem to be his preferences." He flagged down a hansom, and they climbed in. Hodgins got out at the corner of Yonge and King Streets, instructing the driver to take Harrington to the docks.

After hours of searching, the closest they came was finding a few women who knew him. Unfortunately, none had any idea where he might be.

One by one they returned to the station, first Harrington, then Hodgins, each looking tired, frustrated, and dejected. Hodgins walked into his office and dropped his little notebook on his desk.

Harrington followed him, but didn't enter. "Sir? We're not giving up, are we?"

The detective sighed and slumped onto his chair. "No. Just feeling lost. Sit. Maybe if we put our heads together, we can come up with something. Tobias is about your age. Where would you go to think things over?"

"Well, I'd talk things through with my father."

Hodgins shook his head. "The little contact I've had with Mr. Hinds left me with the impression he's not someone who'd consider his son's feelings or opinion. And Mrs. Hinds seems to still think of him as a child."

"Friends?"

"Doesn't appear he had any."

Harrington grinned. "Telling his woes over a pint? Maybe we just didn't find the right tavern."

"The city has its fair share. My feet won't take much more walking right now. Maybe with our bellies full, we'll have more energy. Let's go to Rossin House. My treat. We can review the list of places we've hit and make a list of the ones still left."

"Lunch at Rossin House? It's rather fancy."

Hodgins stood. "We deserve a treat. Come on."

By the time they arrived, it was almost two. Harrington stared up at the five-storey building at the corner of King and York Streets. "Are you sure they'll let me in dressed in uniform? I feel like I should be wearing a waistcoat and top hat."

"Nonsense. They'll take my money. Been in here a few times with the wife. Besides, I know a few of the staff from primary school. Some of their childhood pranks would cost them their jobs." Hodgins clapped Harrington on the back. "There's something you must see before we go to the restaurant."

He led the constable to the interior courtyard. Harrington stood, mouth open, staring at the lush garden and babbling fountain.

Hodgins grinned, practically having to drag Harrington back out. When they entered the restaurant, the maître d' looked down his nose at them.

"You must be lost."

Hodgins held up his hand, stopping him before he could say anything further. "No, we're here for lunch. If there's a problem, I'm certain Christopher can straighten it out. You do know Chris Lakefield?"

The maître d' raised an eyebrow. "Mr. Lakefield? The manager?"

"Yes, that's the one. Shall I have my friend here find him, or do you want to fetch him yourself?" Hodgins turned to Harrington. "Why don't you go to the check-in desk and ask for him?"

"No need to bother him, I'm sure." The snobby employee was dumfounded but waved over a waiter. "Show these gentlemen to a table."

"Certainly." The waiter shook Hodgins' hand. "Nice to see you again, Albert. Got a good spot by the window."

The three of them walked into the restaurant, leaving a shocked maître d' at the entrance.

After finishing their meal of roast pork, they got down to business. Hodgins and Harrington compared notes on which areas they'd checked and made a list of streets with possible places Tobias might attend, agreeing to meet at the station house by five o'clock.

When Hodgins arrived back shortly after five, Harrington sat at his desk chatting with Riddell. He joined them. "Any luck?"

"No, sir. He's just vanished."

"I've had little luck tracking the mysterious doctor as well." Riddell's eyes were puffy from reading the old newspapers for most of the day.

"Can't have all the criminals simply let themselves get caught. Put us out of a job. Cases like this give us a much needed challenge." Hodgins looked around. "Any word from Barnes?"

"Saw him briefly mid-morning." Riddell sat forward, leaning on his walking stick. "Checked in with the sarge before getting a fresh horse to continue his search. Said no one he spoke to yesterday saw Lenny Brown."

"Blast. I'll leave word for Barnes not to bother going out again tomorrow. Hopefully, I'll get in before he does. If he's not found the trail after two days of searching, it'll have gone cold." He checked his pocket watch. "It's ten past five. Head home. Get a good night's sleep. We'll all put our heads together at eight-thirty tomorrow morning. There's got to be something we're missing."

CHAPTER ELEVEN

Hodgins arrived early and found a note on his desk from Barnes.

Located Brown. Will fill you in in the morning.

He went to the front to ask the desk sergeant if he knew anything more. "Did he tell you any details?"

"Yes. Palmer filled me in before I relieved him this morning. Barnes came in around midnight, all excited about finding someone who recognized the photograph of Brown. Apparently, he was disappointed when he gave him your instructions not to go back out today."

Hodgins nodded. "I'm sure he was. If he has located Brown, I don't want him, or anyone, going out alone to bring him in."

Henry was the first of the constables to arrive. Hodgins noticed the heavy bags under the constable's eyes as he headed to the detective's office with as much energy as he could manage.

"Sit before you fall over. I found the note you left me. Where did you find him?" Hodgins had his pencil poised, ready to add the details to his own notes.

Barnes flopped onto the chair and leaned back. "Not that far past Leslieville. He's somewhere around Norway. Clerk at the general store recognized him. Rode like the wind to get back." He smiled weakly. "I'll bet Thunder is still sleeping."

Hodgins raised an eyebrow. "Mitchell gave you Thunder? He's a little hard to handle."

"Only one he had available. He's not so tough after yesterday. Good thing Mitchell told us where his hidden key is. I gave the horse a good brushing. He was asleep before I finished. Didn't even bother with his feed and water."

"We'll all go out to find Lenny. Tom and Floyd are meeting us here at eight-thirty to plan the next steps for Miss Dickson's killer, but it can wait another day. We need to find the child first." Hodgins checked the time. "Should be arriving soon." He looked up when the front door to the station opened. "Here they are now."

Riddell and Harrington carried in chairs and sat beside Barnes.

Riddell gave Barnes the once over. "You look a fright. Been up to no good, Henry?" He chuckled and nudged Henry's arm.

"If finding the baby napper is no good, then yes, I've been up to no good."

Harrington's face lit up. "Little Alfie's been found? He's okay?"

Hodgins held up his hands. "Don't get too excited. We haven't got him yet. He's been spotted, though. So, change of plans. Instead of hashing out ideas on how to find Tobias Hinds, we're all going to Norway to find and arrest Lenny Brown and his wife. No one is to mention it, just in case we can't find him. Don't want to get anyone's hopes up."

Harrington looked puzzled. "Norway? How did Barnes get all the way there and back so fast?"

The detective laughed. "Not the country. There's a little settlement east of here. Only been around a few years. Can't be many people there. A stranger would be noticed." He turned to Barnes. "See if Mitchell has that buggy you borrowed for the twins' party available. I'll get the rifles, and hope we don't have to use them."

* * *

Just over thirty minutes later, the officers found the village of Norway and Frank Boston's mercantile. A few tiny homes sat scattered along the only road through town, likely built as people settled. Hodgins tied the horse to a hitching post and went in with Barnes. The other constables stretched their legs outside. As they were outside the city boundary, they were allowed to remove their helmets and open the top button of their uniform.

"Morning, sir. Remember me?" Barnes shook hands with the proprietor. "We've come to find Mr. Brown and his family."

Boston glanced at Hodgins' badge. "Not in any trouble, are they? He wasn't the most friendly chap to come into my store."

"We need to find them for a little chat." Hodgins flashed his finest smile. "Any idea where they might have headed?"

"Well, he bought a tent and some cooking things. She got flour, eggs, and milk. Not enough to last long, so I don't suppose they got far." Mr. Boston nodded towards the front window. "Those fellas hanging around out there with you?"

"Yes. Please don't mention this to anyone. We just want to quietly find them."

"They went east. That's about all I kin tell ya. Like I said, he weren't the friendly type."

They all piled back into the wagon and continued east, out of view of the settlement. Only a few farms were visible near the town. They rode in silence for twenty minutes, then Barnes called out.

"There." He pointed to his left. "Looks like someone rode through the bush recently."

Hodgins slowed the horse and tugged the reins left. Once the wagon was up the trail and out of sight of the road, he stopped.

"We walk from here. If the tracks are from Brown, I don't want him hearing us. Tom, you able to manage the bush with the walking stick? Maybe you should stay with the wagon. Back her out and wait on the road."

Riddell looked down, kicking at the ground. "Much as I'd like to join you, I don't want to slow you down. If they make a break for it, I'll be ready to chase."

"Good lad. Mitchell would have my hide if someone came along, found an empty wagon, and made off with it."

As Riddell slowly backed the wagon to the road, Hodgins, Barnes, and Harrington followed the ruts into the bush.

They'd only walked for five minutes when Hodgins stopped. "Hold up. You smell that?"

Both constables sniffed the air. In unison, they whispered. "Campfire."

They crept along until Hodgins spotted a small clearing. "I see them. We can approach from behind the tent. Ready?"

"Ready."

"Ready."

The sun sat overhead, so no long shadows were cast. Inside the tent, a woman sang to a giggling child. Riddell and Harrington edged around the right side of the tent, Hodgins went left.

A twig snapped under the detective's foot. He stood frozen, hoping the trees hid him. His heart pounded in his ears. Hodgins closed his eyes and took a deep breath to calm his nerves, releasing it slowly.

Brown turned and called out. "Is someone there? Show yourself."

Now or never. Hodgins stepped out of hiding. "Lenny Brown, you're under arrest for child snatching."

"You'll never catch me." Brown bolted off before Hodgins could raise his rifle.

The detective took off after him. Brown made no attempt to mask his footfalls, allowing Hodgins to follow the thudding and snapping of twigs. Twice, Hodgins paused to catch his breath. *Should've let one of the constables do the chasing.* He caught a glimpse of movement through the trees to his right and turned. "Brown, stop. We have your wife." *I hope.* "You can't get away. There's no place to hide in the woods. Give yourself up."

"Never! You'll—"

A crash followed by a string of cussing resonated through the tress. Hodgins ran towards the sound. Lenny had tripped over an exposed root. The detective raised his rifle and approached the fallen man. "You were saying?"

Brown tried to stand, but couldn't. "I think I busted my ankle."

"Well, I'm not going to carry you." Hodgins looked around and found a four-foot branch nearby, thick enough to support his prisoner's weight. "Use this." He tossed it to Brown, then stood back, rifle cocked and aimed. "Get moving or I'll leave you for the coyotes." Sweat stung Hodgins' eyes. He leaded against a tree, taking advantage of a break in the chase and wiped his brow.

They walked single file back to the camp, Hodgins staying just far enough back to avoid Brown swinging the branch at him. When they got back, Harrington stood with the baby.

Hodgins continued to aim his rifle at the criminal while Barnes cuffed Lenny.

"We didn't steal nothing." Lenny spat on the ground near Hodgins' feet. "Kid's kin. Belongs with his own."

"Afraid not. The child was born here, in prison. His mother will never be released, and his father is dead. You have no claim. He won't be handed over to a pack of criminals. He has a new family now. *I hope.*"

As they loaded the couple into the back of their own wagon, both Browns spewed out one vile comment after another. Barnes sat in the back with them after tying Mrs. Brown's hands with rope. Alfie had fallen asleep, so Harrington set him on the wagon bench before helping Hodgins put out the fire and pack up the tent and the few items lying around. After hitching the horse, Hodgins drove the Brown's wagon out along the trail, with Harrington beside him holding Alfie on his lap.

When they reached the road, Harrington and the baby joined Riddell, and they followed the detective back to Toronto.

* * *

Hodgins put Lenny in one cell, his wife in the adjoining one. "I hope no one else from your family tries snatching the child. Whoever takes him in will be given his full history so the parents can made certain he's safe."

Lenny grabbed the bars. "You'd better hope he's with someone who knows how to handle a gun. He's a Brown. The family won't stop looking for him."

Mrs. Brown moved to the bars separating her from her husband. "You just wait 'til The Butcher gets released. Whoever has Alfie will find a knife in their gut before he can reach for a gun." She spewed out more profanities, some Hodgins had never heard.

The detective left a constable to watch over the prisoners and went back to the front of the station. Most of the constables stood crowded around one desk. Harrington still had Alfie, and everyone was checking to make certain the child was unharmed.

"Barnes, on your way home make sure you return the wagon Brown bought from Dominion Livery."

"Yes, sir. No doubt he'll be glad to get it back. What if he inquires about returning the money to Brown?"

Hodgins shrugged. "Tell him to keep it. Brown won't be needing it where he's going."

"And Alfie?" Harrington bounced the baby on his knee.

"Don't get too comfortable, Floyd. We can't keep him." Hodgins peered over Barnes' shoulder, smiling.

"Yes, sir. I know. But what's going to happen to him?"

Hodgins shrugged. "I'm going to see if the Throckmorton's have changed their minds. If not, he'll have to go back to the Protestant's Orphan Home. Someone will want him. Don't suppose you'd care to mind him a little longer?

Harrington gave a grin so wide it almost touched his ears. "Take all the time you need."

CHAPTER TWELVE

When Hodgins arrived at the Throckmorton's, he found Otis sitting on the veranda, reading the newspaper. The detective walked over and leaned on the railing. "Afternoon. I have word on the child. I'd like to speak with you and your wife about him."

Otis folded the paper. "I thought I made myself clear. We do not wish to raise the child of a murderer. I had my lawyer look into the family. Murderers and thieves, the lot of them. No. We discussed it and gave you our answer. I would appreciate it if you didn't bother us again."

"But he's just a child. He knows nothing of his parents or their family. You don't honestly believe he's inherited murderous traits?"

Otis opened his newspaper and continued reading. "G'day, detective."

Angry, Hodgins stood his ground. "Now, see here. You can't be serious. You've a responsibility."

Mr. Throckmorton didn't reply. The curtain in the window moved and Hodgins spotted Alice. She shook her head, then let the curtain drop back into place.

"If that's the way you feel, Alfie is much better off elsewhere. Good day." The detective stormed off, muttering words he'd never say in front of his wife.

When he arrived at the station, most of the constables were back at work. Harrington sat at his desk, going through old copies of the city directory, Alfie on his lap. He looked up when the detective walked over. "From the look on your face, they haven't changed their minds."

"No. Afraid not, Floyd. He's better off somewhere else, anyway. It's time to take him back to the home. Why don't you come along? He's taken a shine to you. Too bad you aren't married. You'd give him a good home." Hodgins lifted the basket containing Alfie's belongings. "We'll exchange Mitchell's wagon for a carriage. Take him back in style."

* * *

After dropping off the child and returning the carriage, Hodgins sent a dejected-looking Harrington home, then stopped briefly at Station Four. Barnes and Riddell were looking at a photograph. Both seemed to be in good spirts. Silently, he walked up behind them. "You still here? What are you looking at?"

Both constables jumped.

"Gracious, sir. You gave us a fright." Barnes passed the photo to the detective.

Hodgins grinned. "Lovely photograph of Floyd and Alfie. Is this what the department purchased all that equipment for?"

Riddell had a ready reply. "Why, it's evidence we found the boy, and he's safe."

"Right. And I suppose it's best kept in the protective care of Harrington?" Hodgins' grin widened.

Catching on they weren't in trouble, Barnes spoke up. "Won't be necessary. We made an extra copy. Good practice for Tom."

"Good thinking." Hodgins slapped Barnes on the back. "I have a feeling it will take quite some time for him to get over the lad." He took out his pocket watch. "Your shifts are almost over." He dug a few coins from his pocket. "Run out and find a frame for the picture. I'm certain Floyd would enjoy that."

* * *

Once home, Hodgins filled Cordelia in on the return of Alfie. "Good thing we managed to sneak up on his camp. We caught him off guard and he took off running, but no one was injured except Brown. Lenny's wife certainly has quite the unladylike vocabulary. I hope the boy doesn't remember any of it."

"It's a shame he had to go back to the home." Cordelia sighed. "Maybe one day the girls will discover they have a brother."

Hodgins nodded. "Unfortunately, next time I won't know who takes Alfie. Matron made that clear. I did strongly suggest she tell the boy's background to whoever takes him."

"I'm lunching with Amelia tomorrow and will ask her if she can see his future."

Hodgins reached over and patted Delia's hand. "Yes, dear. Why don't you do that?"

After the evening meal, the Hodgins' family went into the backyard to enjoy the lovely early spring weather. The twins dug in the dirt, watched over by big sister Sara. Scraps lay between Hodgins and Delia, dozing. Without warning, the dog leapt up and raced to the fence separating their property from the Holiwell's.

When Henry and Violet married, a portion of fence was removed so guests could wander both lawns. They took several wedding photographs under the apple tree on the Hodgins property, as it was in full bloom. When they replaced the fence boards weeks later, Hodgins built a gate to allow easy access between the properties. Scraps had his paws on the gate, tail wagging rapidly. Henry Barnes leaned over and gave the dog a pat.

"Evening, sir. Mind if we join you?" Henry turned when his father-in-law joined him at the fence.

"Please, come in. Where are your wives?"

Henry reached over and lifted the latch. "Talking about dresses." Barnes made a face. "Don't know how they find so much to talk about. Say, why don't you join them, Mrs. Hodgins? They value your opinion."

Cordelia stood. "I think I will. You'll probably bore me with whatever you men talk about." She called to her oldest daughter. "Sara, mind the girls." She made sure to latch the gate tightly behind her.

Mr. Halloway sat in the chair vacated by Cordelia, and Barnes sat on the step, leaning back against the house.

"Henry was telling us about that child that was taken. Glad he's been found. Just awful his new family doesn't want him back. Just awful." Mr. Halloway tsk-ed and shook his head.

"Couldn't agree more, but if that's their attitude, he's better off somewhere else." Hodgins glanced at Barnes. "Say, maybe you and Violet could take him?"

"He's a cute enough fellow, but Violet wants to try for our own first. We actually spoke of it before dinner."

Mr. Halloway tapped Hodgins' arm. "Say, old chap, since you have his sisters—"

"Stop right there. We've already discussed it, more than once. I agree it would be ideal, but it's just not practical. Maybe one of Delia's acquaintances would consider. Even if they never found out they're siblings, at least they'd know each other. We have more pressing things to think about. We still haven't captured the person responsible for Miss Dickson's death."

Not wishing to hear the details of the murder, Mr. Halloway changed the subject to more mundane things. He was an amateur botanist and Hodgins enjoyed their talks about plants.

Over an hour passed before Cordelia returned with instructions to send their guests back home. Sara had taken the twins up to bed already and remained upstairs, studying.

"It's getting chilly, Bertie. Nice cup of tea beside the fireplace?" Cordelia stood on the back step.

Hodgins opened door and Scraps bounded through, followed by Delia. "Sounds lovely, but as your father would say, I'll have mine with a touch of Irish."

* * *

The next morning, shortly after Hodgins settled behind his office desk, Riddell came in. "Sir? I believe I found something."

Hodgins put down his notebook. "Sit. Is it to do with the death of Miss Jackson?"

Riddell nodded. "Never did find the doctor sent when Coward was unavailable. Apparently, he doesn't exist."

The detective leaned back, grinning. "Doesn't exist? The landlady and her maid both saw him. Was he a specter?"

"Well, the man exists. It's just that he's not exactly a doctor. One of the reporters at *The Globe* has also been trying to find him. He's been practicing quackery."

"A charlatan? Didn't we run one out of town last fall? Why haven't I heard of another selling his useless medicines?"

"This one is an odd duck, pardon the pun. Instead of selling his elixirs, he's been offering his services to physicians. I don't believe any complaints have been made as the patients didn't realize he's not a licensed doctor. The reporter only found out when a neighbour mentioned becoming worse after he administered medicine. The regular physician attended, and she got better."

Hodgins threw his pencil down on the desk. "Nothing more than a criminal. Why would an honest doctor hire such a person? Did you get a name?"

"Yes. Doctor Clover. The regular physician was Doctor Traybar. His name came up once already, but seems he's moved away."

Hodgins stood. "Good work. I need to find out the name of the first doctor to attend Miss Jackson. If it was this Clover person, he may be responsible for her death. Maybe others as well. A visit to Coward's office is in order. Care to join me?"

Their first stop was at the ladies' boarding house. The maid answered the door, looking an absolute mess. Her white apron and cap were covered in soot. A number of hair pins had come loose, allowing several strands of hair to hang over her eyes. Hodgins recalled how the temperature had dropped over night and he'd lit a fire in all the bedrooms. The ladies in the lodgings wouldn't have the luxury of a spring fire in their rooms unless they paid extra for the coal.

He smiled as she tucked the few stray hairs back under her cap and adjusted her pins. "Messy job, cleaning the hearth. Guess I'll be doing that tonight, too."

She smiled back, then took the detective and constable to the sitting room, quickly rushing off to find the landlady. Hodgins noticed the freshly cleaned fireplace, not a speck of soot remaining. *Probably more on the maid than in the bucket.* Mrs. Holiwell joined them less than a minute later.

"Detective, have you discovered the killer? People are already gossiping, saying my house isn't safe for young ladies."

"We're still piecing together the information we've gathered. I just have one more question for you. Could you tell me the name of the physician Doctor Coward sent in his place?"

She nodded. "Yes. I remember his name, as it suited him. Doctor Clover. He was sweet as clover, and quite handsome. A real charmer. Say, he hasn't done nothing wrong, has he?"

"Aside from practicing medicine without a license? I don't know, yet." He tipped his homburg. "Good day."

Riddell made a quick note in his book and followed Hodgins out. As they made their way to Doctor Cowards' office by the docks, the detective mumbled, partially to himself, partially to his constable. "Doesn't he realize how much harm he could do? Does he even care? Ought to be in jail."

"Don't worry, sir. We'll catch him."

CHAPTER THIRTEEN

By the time they reached their destination, both men were fuming, and Riddell's limp had magnified noticeably. Hodgins reached for the handle and found it unlocked. "He's in. Lucky for me. Not so lucky for him."

The door to what might have been an examination room sat ajar. The voices indicated the doctor was with a patient. Riddell looked around while Hodgins stood by the only window in the room, facing the street. The view was unimpressive, partially obscured by grime. A few minutes later, the exam door opened fully and a burly man exited, followed by Coward. The man's forearm sported a goodly amount of gauze wrapping, covering most of his skin from wrist to elbow.

Coward nodded at Hodgins, then glanced at Riddell. "Please don't touch anything."

Once they were alone, Hodgins couldn't hold his tongue any longer. "How could you be so irresponsible? Do you know how much harm he could inflict?"

Coward waved both hands in front of him, narrowing his eyes. "Hold on. What exactly are you accusing me of?"

"Doctor Clover. Or should I say *mister* Clover? How could you work with that charlatan?"

The doctor relaxed. "Ah, I see. Yes, I understand your anger. He's no longer associated with my practice. One of the hospitals he listed as a reference just happens to be the same hospital a colleague works at. I wrote to him and mentioned Clover. Just heard back yesterday that no such person worked there. I immediately sent a telegram to his school." Coward went to his desk and retrieved the reply. "Read it yourself. He attended for less than a year, then left. You just missed him, actually. Fired him less than an hour ago."

Hodgins read the letter, then handed it to Riddell. "So he has some medical knowledge, but not a degree."

"I thought maybe he went to another school, even though he didn't list another. When I asked him, he just shrugged and said it was nice while it lasted. I doubt he's qualified to do little more than bandage a simple wound, like the dock worker who just left. Most of my clients are sailors and dock workers with only minor injuries. They often refer me to family and friends."

Hodgins pulled out his notebook and flipped to the page listing the other deceased ladies. "Were any of these women patients of yours?"

The doctor read the names. "Well, you already know I saw Miss Jackson shortly before she died. Don't recognize the others. Let me check." He rummaged through his files for ten minutes. "No, I have no files for any of them. Are you thinking Clover may have had something to do with their deaths? I assume those other ladies are deceased?"

"Yes. Clover was a possibility. Was he working here between September and now?"

"No. He was only here about two months. Said he came in from Kingston. Of course, he may have lied about that."

Hodgins snapped his notebook shut. "I still have another avenue of inquiry to follow up on. If you hear anything of his whereabouts, please send word."

Riddell scribbled most of the conversation in his book, then gave the letter back to the doctor. Hodgins sent the constable to the station alone on the trolley, then walked north, ending up at the Horticulture Gardens on Gerrard Street. He sat on a bench and thumbed through his notes, attempting to determine if there was a connection between all the deaths his constables discovered.

Clover would have had access to the quicksilver, but he wasn't in the city for several of the deaths. Difficult to confirm. The missing

Tobias had access to it, but quantities needed are not missing. Why has he gone into hiding? Is he really hiding, or has something happened to him?

He sighed heavily, then stood, stretching out his back. In order to clear his mind, he wandered the five acres, enjoying the early spring blooms. For the next thirty minutes, he chatted with several people, also enjoying the spring weather, then headed back to Station Four.

As he ambled down Parliament, he spotted Barnes walking up. Hodgins waited for the constable at Wilton Avenue and together they headed to the station.

Hodgins noticed Barnes flipping through his notebook and hoped for good news. "Any update on our missing man?"

Barnes shrugged. "I tracked down some acquaintances of the deceased women. Wanted to see if any of them knew Mr. Hinds."

"Get their addresses from the arrest reports?"

Barnes gave the detective a lopsided grin. "Yes, sir. Seems Tobias availed himself of their services, but wasn't particularly attracted to any of the ones I spoke to. Just the ones who've died. One lady did mention he was partial to drink."

Hodgins opened the front door of the station, letting Barnes in first. "Did a pretty good job of asking around the taverns with Harrington. No one remembers seeing him. We concentrated on the area around the docks and several blocks north. We'd better expand to the outlying areas. Fewer taverns, but it's worth checking."

The detective flipped through the directory for the addresses of the establishments closer to the city boundaries, then headed back out with Harrington. It took over two hours before anyone admitted Tobias Hinds had been in their tavern.

"Yeah, he was here." The bartender handed back the sketch of the missing man. "Had ta toss him out on his arse. Started three fights with blokes twice his size. Laughable, really. Couldn't lay a finger on the big guys. Everyone laughed, which made him madder. Fists swinging like a windmill, but never hit anything. Only reason I tossed him was 'cause he started throwing chairs. Can't afford to replace stuff every time there's a fight."

Hodgins passed the sketch to Harrington, then turned back to the bartender. "I doubt the family can make restitution, but maybe they can come to an arrangement with you. Now, how long ago did you toss him?"

"Hmm, let me think." He scratched his scruffy beard. "Can't be more than an hour ago. If he had any sense, he went home to sleep it off."

Someone tapped a coin on the far end of the bar, catching the bartender's attention. "Customer." He left Hodgins and Harrington with no further comment.

"Seems like we've been dismissed. Let's hope Tobias took his advice and went home. Don't think we'll find a hansom in this part of town. Trolley shouldn't be too far." Hodgins moved towards the door. "You get off close to the station house. I'll continue to the Hinds."

Half way to the Hind's residence, Harrington spotted Tobias, stumbling down the middle of the street, holding up the flow of traffic. Drivers of carriages, wagons, and cabriolets yelled one after the other.

Hodgins nudged Harrington. "We'd better grab him before the situation gets out of control."

Together, they jumped off the trolley and ran the half block to the cause of the problem, carefully avoiding the horse dung. Several cheers went up as the officers guided the young drunk onto the nearest lawn. Many flung one final insult.

When most of the backlog had cleared, someone called out. "Need a hand, Bert?"

Hodgins turned, recognizing the driver. "Charlie. You have a customer?"

"Nope. Just let them off around the corner. Where ya headed?" Charlie stopped his horse at the curb beside Hodgins.

"Drop Harrington at the station, then take me and my drunk friend to Sumach Street. Help us get him up, will ya?"

Tobias was half-way in the hansom when he began retching.

"Not in my cab." Charlie grabbed Tobias' trousers and pulled him back. "Whew, that was close."

Unfortunately, a lady and her child walked by just as Hinds threw up in the street. The little girl screamed. The lady gave them a look that would turn milk sour and hurried away.

"You have a shovel, Charlie?" Hodgins chuckled lightly.

"Always." Charlie untied a shovel from the back of the hansom. "Fares in the high-class areas don't like it when the horse does what nature demands. Want the bucket, too?"

Hodgins shook his head. "No. Harrington, get a shovelful of dirt off the road and cover it. Mind you don't leave a hole for a wheel to catch on or horse to stumble."

It only took a few minutes to cover the mess on the road. Charlie tied the shovel back in place and, with his fare in the cabriolet, guided the horse to the police station.

When Charlie stopped to let the constable off, Harrington turned to the detective. "He's quite a mess. Should we clean him up some before his mother sees him?"

"No. I think it's time she gets a good look at her beloved son for what he really is. Actually, on second thought, let him spend the night in a cell. He's a murder suspect and publicly drunk."

Hodgins tore a page from his notebook and wrote a brief note. "Charlie, deliver this, will you? Let the family know where he is." He paid Charlie double the fare, then helped escort the lad to a cell.

Tobias fell asleep immediately, face down on the small bed.

"You head home, Floyd. I'll stay and wait. I expect one or both parents will arrive within the next thirty minutes or so."

While he waited, the detective stood by the sergeant's desk, inquiring about the little orphan girl he and his wife took in six months earlier.

Sergeant Cooper grinned. "Oh, little Sally has settled in nicely. After living on the street for a year, wearing the same dress every day, she was proud to wear some of my Betsy's hand-me-downs. You should've seen her face when she got a brand new dress. And she's ever so clever. Doing well in school. Betsy helps with her homework. She loves her new little sister."

"Too bad you and your family couldn't make it to the twin's party. My wife would love to meet Sally."

A ruckus outside the station interrupted the conversation. Hodgins opened the door and almost collided with Mrs. Hinds. Her husband stood by the cabriolet, paying Charlie for the ride to the station. Charlie gave Hodgins a nod and continued on.

Mrs. Hinds stormed past the detective and bellowed at no one in particular. "Where's my baby? What have you done with him? I demand you release him at once."

Her husband came in and tried to quiet her. "We're here now. Settle down and we'll sort it out." Hinds turned to Hodgins. "Can we see him now and take him home?"

"It might be best if you wait until morning before you see him."

"Nonsense. Where's Tobias? His mother is in a state. Why is he in jail? Has he been arrested?"

Hodgins waved him over to an empty desk. "He's drunk. Started a fight at a saloon on Louisa Street, near Trinity Square. Broke several chairs. Threw up in the street. He's sleeping it off."

Hinds signed. "Yes, let him sleep it off. Might do his mother some good to see him, though."

The detective agreed and took them to the cells.

Mrs. Hinds pulled out her kerchief and covered her nose and mouth. "Don't you ever clean in here? Disgusting! What have you done to my baby?" As soon as she spotted Tobias, she dropped her kerchief and grabbed hold of the bars, calling to her son. "Tobias! Toby dear!"

"We've done nothing to him, ma'am. I can assure you he did that to himself. He's three sheets to the wind. Puked in the street. Why don't you come back tomorrow after work?"

"Drunk? No, not my boy. Tobias, you know how I feel about drinking. You'll ruin any chance of finding a nice girl and settling down." She droned on for several minutes on the evil of drink before her husband pulled her away from the cell.

For the first time since meeting her, Mrs. Hinds had run out of words. She allowed her husband to escort her out. Once they left, Hodgins gave instructions for someone to check on Tobias regularly in case he was sick again, then went home.

* * *

After supper, as the weather was especially pleasant, the entire family walked to the Ketchum schoolyard so Scraps could have a good run. A few of Sara's classmates were there, so she joined them. Too young to keep up with the older children, Holly and Ivy chased the dog. The detective and his wife sat on the school steps to enjoy the breeze.

Cordelia filled him in on the gossip she'd heard while out shopping. "The Greene's are planning a trip to Italy this summer. Their son is married now, and they have no pressing commitments. Harold Junior will take care of the business while they're gone." She heaved a heavy sign. "Sometimes I wish you had a more regular job so we can go places."

Hodgins put his arm around her shoulders. "I know exactly how you feel. Once school lets out, I'll request a week's leave and take the family to Lake Superior on the Northern Railway. Take one of the steamboat excursions. It's not Italy, but it is nice."

"Our first real outing with the twins. Marvelous. Anywhere will be perfect, just as long as we're together." She turned to look at him. "You can leave your work behind, can't you?"

He patted her hand. "Of course. You are quite the distraction. Since we're gossiping, have you heard from Amelia lately? Stonehouse has been noticeably absent, and as they've been keeping company, maybe she's mentioned him?"

"I saw her a few days ago for lunch. When I inquired after the doctor, she said very little." Cordelia gasped. "Oh,

Bertie. You don't think they had an argument and parted company?"

"None of our business, Delia. Could explain why he's staying away. Even when I don't require news from the coroner, he generally stops by for a quick chat. Maybe he's uncomfortable speaking to me about it, seeing as they met through us."

"I so enjoy her friendship. I do hope whatever it is doesn't ruin that."

Sara rushed around the corner of the building. "Mamma, Pappa. I think it's time to leave. Holly and Ivy have fallen asleep." She smiled. "Scraps is laying with them."

Hodgins stood and helped Cordelia up. "Maybe in another fifteen or twenty years we can grab more than thirty minutes alone."

CHAPTER FOURTEEN

The first thing Hodgins did that morning after arriving at the Station House was check on young Hinds. He found Tobias sitting on the side of the bed, head in hands.

"Rough night, son?"

Tobias slowly raised his head, looking up at Hodgin's through blood-shot eyes. "If you're here to lecture me on the evils of drink, my mother said everything possible last night. Just pretended to be sleeping, hoping she'd stop talking." He ran a hand through his hair, making it stand up more than before. "Can I go home now?"

"Afraid not. We need to have a little chat." Hodgins motioned to the constable with him to unlock the cell, then led Tobias to the interrogation room, stopping long enough to ask another constable to fetch a strong cup of tea for his prisoner.

Once Tobias had several gulps, he looked a little more alert.

Hodgins wasted no time questioning him. "Why did you run off? Feeling guilty about killing Miss Jackson?"

"What? No. I didn't kill her. I loved her."

"So, why run?"

"I don't know. It just finally got to me. All the questions, the grief. My mother treating me like a child."

"Hmm." Hodgins opened his notebook. "What about Alice Marshall? Emma Stokes? Ellen Davies? You courted each of them, and they're all dead. Just like Annabel Jackson. Killed with quicksilver."

Tobias squinted at the detective, barely able to keep his head up. "I don't understand. Do you believe they were murdered? The police said it was accidental poisoning."

"Bit of a coincidence, don't you think? You court someone, they reject you, and then they end up dead. Poisoned with something easily obtained at your position with the pharmacy."

"No!" Tobias waved his arms, knocking over the half-full teacup. "Why would I kill them? Yes, each rejected my proposal, but I quickly found another. There was no reason to murder any of them."

"Unless you can prove you had nothing to do with it, you'll be staying here. It doesn't look good for you. Don't imagine the trial will take long. Plenty of reason to believe you're guilty, and not one reason to think you're innocent."

Hodgins stood and walked to the door. "You'll be staying here a while longer." He opened the door, addressing the constable standing guard in the hall. "Take him back to the cell." He watched as Hinds rose and shuffled to the door, back slumped, hollering his innocence.

Tobias Hinds' screams of disbelief echoed through the building. Barnes walked over to the detective's office. "Sir, have you arrested him for Miss Jackson's murder?"

"Yes, and the murders of the other women Harrington and Riddell found. I suppose I'd best let his parents know." Hodgins checked the time. "His father is likely already at work. Not looking forward to telling Mrs. Hinds. Better get it over with."

* * *

When Hodgins arrived at the Hinds' home, Mrs. Hinds answered the door. The lines around her eyes had deepened since his last visit. She stepped out and looked around. "Where is Tobias? Why haven't you brought him home?"

"I need a word with you. Is your husband still here?"

She shook her head. "He left almost an hour ago. I insist you go away and fetch Toby."

"What about your maid?"

"We're not rich. She only comes in twice weekly. Tell me why you've come."

"May we speak inside?"

After one more look around for her son, she allowed the detective entry.

"I do wish there was someone with you. I'm afraid the news is distressing. We have arrested your son for the murder of Miss Jackson, and three other women."

Mrs. Hinds stared, then began to waver. Afraid she would faint, Hodgins quickly guided her into the sitting room and to the nearest chair.

"Is there a neighbour who could sit with you?"

Her eyes widened. "The neighbours can't know. What will they think?"

They'll read it in the newspaper soon enough. "A family member then?"

"My sister." The address given wasn't far from Hodgins' home.

"I have a hansom waiting. I'll take you over."

The shock set in on the way over, and by the time they arrived, Mrs. Hines had totally shut down. The sister had a full-time maid and immediately sent her to fetch both a doctor and her husband. Hodgins instructed the hansom driver to take her wherever she said, then to return for him.

He explained the situation once the maid departed and Mrs. Hinds settled in the guest room on the second floor.

"Surely you can't believe Tobias would do such a horrible thing? His mother does coddle him, but that wouldn't lead him to murder! My husband will provide a lawyer. The best."

Over an hour passed before the maid returned with Mr. Crater. The doctor had come and gone, leaving sleeping tablets for Mrs. Hinds.

"Thank you for bringing her to us." Mr. Crater shook Hodgins' hand. "I tried to get Hinds to come, but he said there was nothing he could do if the boy had been arrested. My wife's sister didn't marry well, as you've no doubt noticed. He's not a cruel man. Just uneducated. He provides the best he can."

"For the lad's sake, I hope your lawyer can find proof of his innocence. The evidence, while only circumstantial, is damning. It doesn't look good at all. He's at Station Four on Wilton Street. I'll leave you to take care of Mrs. Hinds."

Along the way back, Hodgins stopped at Elliot's to inform Tobias' employer not to expect the young man to return to work. Elliot could let his employees know. When the driver let him off at the station, Hodgins gave him a generous tip for all the extra running around. Shortly before going home for the day, a lawyer came in to speak with Tobias Hinds. The detective directed one of the constables to show him to the cell, then headed home.

For once, Hodgins was in no mood to discuss the case with Cordelia. He told her that Tobias had been arrested, then headed to his favourite spot in the chair by the fireplace, whisky in one hand, newspaper in the other, Scraps curled at his feet.

CHAPTER FIFTEEN

Over the next three days, the lawyer came and went regularly. Unfortunately, for young Hinds, no alibi could be found for the times of any of the women's murders. The newspapers were filled with the story, half of the details totally made up to sell papers. A trial date was set for the coming Tuesday. Everyone expected a guilty return followed shortly by a hanging.

Mid afternoon Wednesday, Harrington rushed into Hodgins office, panting. "Sir. You won't… won't believe…"

"Sit down. Take a few deep breaths. You look like you're about to pass out."

Harrington dropped onto the empty chair, trying to slow his breathing.

"Better? Now, what won't I believe?"

"It's Gertie… Miss Dickson. I just heard they've rushed her to the hospital. Tried to top herself."

"What? Kill herself? Are you certain? Why would she do such a thing?"

"I was doing my rounds and went by Elliot's to call on her. See if she could break for tea. Thought maybe she'd agree to step out with me Saturday. Go to a dance. Anyway, that's when I heard. Happened Tuesday."

Hodgins thought back to an earlier conversation at Elliot's when one of the clerks mentioned Miss Dickson was sweet on Tobias. *Could she be so distraught she'd consider such drastic measures?*

"I've nothing pressing until the trial. You finish your rounds and I'll go to the hospital. See if she's well enough to chat. Could be she knows something about Mr. Hinds."

Halfway to the hospital, a brief spring shower fell just long enough to settle the dust on the road, but not heavy enough to turn everything to mud. Hodgins entered the building, shook the water droplets off his Homberg, and inquired at the front desk. His footsteps echoed in the empty hallway.

"Good afternoon. Could you give me the room number for Miss Dickson?" He gave the nurse his best smile.

"Are you family?"

"No." Hodgins showed his badge. "I'd like to speak with her. Won't take long."

The young nurse's eyes widened. "You going to arrest her?"

The detective couldn't tell from her expression if she was concerned or felt the way many did about suicide. Both the law and church found an attempt on your own life deplorable.

"No. She needs medical care first. Room, please?"

Her cheeks flushed. "Sorry, sir. Room 305."

Hodgins' footfalls echoed in the hallway. A few nurses entered and exited the wards, carrying trays of medicine or charts. He glanced in before one of the doors closed. A row of beds stood along the exterior wall, under the windows. Each bed was barely two feet from the next. He caught a glimpse of the foot of another row of beds opposite. *Hasn't changed since my last stay almost two years ago.* He hurried up the stairs to the third floor, trying to ignore the moaning and wheezing coming from behind a closed door.

When he entered the room, no family sat with the girl. A middle-aged man stood over her, reading from a bible.

"Excuse me. I don't mean to interrupt, but I need to speak with Miss Dickson. I'm Detective Hodgins."

The man closed the bible and extended a hand. "Reverend Stillwater. She attends services at my church." He glanced at Gertie. "So young. Will she be spending time in jail or in an asylum?"

Hodgins cringed at the mention of the large building on Queen Street West. In 1853, a grand jury investigated the complaints that had been made. Only minor charges were lain, but the rumours stayed in people's minds for years.

"What will happen to her has not been determined. I'd like to hear from Miss Dickson what took place, and why."

"Of course. I have other patients to attend to." The reverend placed a hand on Hodgins' arm. "Be gentle with her. She's a good girl. God Bless." He exited, closing the door behind him.

Hodgins stood beside the bed, looking at the frail figure under the sheet. *Glad her preacher isn't all fire and brimstone.* Gertie turned her head towards the far wall. "Miss Dickson. Gertie. What happened? Is it true? You tried to take your own life? Not an accident?

She nodded slightly.

"But why? You have a good position at Elliot's, friends, family. Is it because Tobias Hinds didn't return your affection? I'd say you're rather lucky, seeing as how his previous sweethearts are all dead."

"You don't understand. He was too good for those trollops. He should have courted me."

Hodgins processed her carefully chosen words. *No. She couldn't mean…*

Gertie turned to face him. "You understand, don't you?"

"Are you saying you're responsible for the deaths of those women?"

"No one will miss them."

"But Miss Jackson was your friend. She had no interest in him. You know that."

"But he still pursued her. I had to make her go away."

"Why are you letting him pay for your crime? You know he'll be hung. If you truly do love him, you won't allow it to come to that."

Gertie smiled, staring off into the distance. "And I'll join him in death. It was meant to be." She closed her eyes. "We'll be together soon, forever."

"I don't believe it works that way, Miss Dickson." He left her room to find the doctor to make sure she didn't try again, then went to the office of Tobias' lawyer.

* * *

The detective was taken aback when he entered the lawyer's office. *Mrs. Hinds' sister must have more money than I thought.* He entered a small outer off with a vacant desk. "Hello? Mrs. Styles?"

"Come in. My secretary had to run some papers over to City Hall." A voice carried through the slightly open door to another office.

Hodgins whistled when he entered. "Very nice. Very nice, indeed." The lawyer sat behind an oak desk in front of a large window. Two leather guest chairs were positioned a foot from the desk.

"Please, have a seat. What can I help you with, detective?"

"I've just come from the hospital. I believe a trial will no longer be necessary." Hodgins relayed his conversation to Mr. Styles. "When I return to the station, I'll prepare a statement and have her sign it. Suggest instead of arresting her, she be committed. She's clearly not in her right mind."

Styles agreed. "I'll speak with the judge. Does this mean Mr. Hinds will be released today?"

"Once the confession is signed. As she's, um, not in her right mind, I'd like to have someone with her when she signs it. I'll speak with her parents. She'll need a lawyer to prepare commitment papers. I'm certain we can release him tomorrow."

Hodgins took his time going back to the station, still trying to process what Gertie had said. *What could possibly have happened to cause that poor woman to behave in such a manner? She was known to the reverend, so she much have faith.* The first thing Hodgins did upon his return was visit Tobias.

"I have some good news, as well as troubling news about Miss Dickson." Hodgins sighed deeply, fetching a chair before telling Tobias what he'd just learned.

"Miss Dickson? Gertie? Has something happened to her? Please don't tell me she's met the same fate as Annabel?"

"No. But she is in the hospital." The detective broke the news about her attempted suicide and confession as gently as possible.

"No. Gertie wouldn't do such a thing. She's very devout. Suicide is a sin." Tobias clasped the bars tight, knuckles white. "A murderess? I've never seen her even a little angry. It… it's not possible."

"According to her, she did. You'll likely be released tomorrow. Just a few details to take care of."

Tobias let go of the bars and staggered backwards, falling onto the small bed. "Four women dead, because of me. I don't know if I should be relieved she confessed, or saddened." He buried his face in his hands, rocking on the side of the bed.

"Both, I expect. I'll leave you to your thoughts."

This is going to be a long night. Hodgins remembered Barnes mentioning earlier he'd be dining at his wife's parents, next door to the Hodgins' home. He found the lad at his desk and asked Henry to let Cordelia know he'd be late. The detective stayed past dark, writing up a statement for Miss Jackson to sign. It took numerous tries to get the wording right.

Finally satisfied, he found the address for Miss Jackson's family and headed over. The house sat in the middle of a row of townhomes. Not a poor family, but not wealthy either. Standing on the tiny porch, he hesitated before knocking. *This has to be the worst part of my job. I'll never get used to it.* He reached out and tapped the knocker twice.

Mr. Jackson answered, standing in the doorway, not inviting him in. Hodgins had no choice but to relay the sad news from the stoop.

Jackson shook his head, unaffected by the news. "We don't wish to discuss our daughter with you. She's brought shame to the family. Now, if you don't mind, we're in the middle of our evening meal." He started to close the door.

Hodgins stopped the door with his hand. "She's confessed to all the murders. You'll need to find a lawyer."

"She's on her own." Jackson shoved the door closed, leaving Hodgins standing on the porch, confused and surprised.

* * *

Cordelia had the same reaction as her husband when he told her about his visit with Miss Jackson's father. "You can't be serious? They've washed their hands of her? I can't imagine anyone doing that. No matter what Sara or the twins did, I'd stand behind them without hesitation."

"As would I. The court will have to appoint someone to handle everything. As she's clearly not in her right mind, I expect she'll be committed to the asylum for the rest of her life, rather than hanging or jail."

A knock sounded on their front door, sending the dog down the hall, barking.

"Whoever could be calling at this hour, Bertie?

He sighed as he rose. "Likely a constable with word of another murder." He called to Scraps as he trudged to the door. "Quiet. Sit."

Scraps obediently sat, tail wagging and thumping on the floor. Hodgins opened the door.

"Miss Alarie! Doctor! What brings you here at this hour? Come into the sitting room." Hodgins called over his shoulder. "Delia, we have guests."

Cordelia hurried from the kitchen and hugged her friend. "Amelia. I haven't heard from you in days." She helped her friend out of her jacket and hung it on the coat tree.

"I could well say the same for you, Doctor. You've been noticeably absent" Hodgins looked from one to the other. "You're both smiling. Come into the sitting room and explain why you're both beaming like school children."

"We have news. Good news." Stonehouse put an arm around Amelia.

"*Oui. Très bien.*" Amelia removed the white lace glove from her left hand. "*Mariée.* We're married."

Cordelia hugged Amelia again, then the doctor. "I'm so happy for you both. Why didn't you say anything?"

"Neither of us wanted a fuss. We had a quiet ceremony and spent a few days in Montreal." Stonehouse accepted the glass of whisky from Hodgins.

"We've come to invite you to a celebration dinner tomorrow. *Les enfants*, too. It will be a double celebration." Amelia looped her arm through her new husband's. "You tell them."

"We've been to the Protestant's Orphan Home to inquire about the boy, Alfie. There's some paperwork to fill out, but we've decided to take him in. He'll grow up knowing his sisters, of course. We'll all have to discuss what we tell them, and when, if you agree. Otherwise, they'll just be friends." He put his arm around Amelia's waist, hugging her tight.

Hodgins clinked glasses with Stonehouse. "Congratulations to you both. Delia and I have had a few discussions about that recently. We agree the girls should know they have a brother. Now they will actually be able to get to know him." Hodgins poured a sherry for Amelia and Cordelia. "It will be complicated."

"Now that we have our drinks, a toast." Cordelia turned to her husband. "Bertie, will you do the honours?"

"Of course. To a long and happy marriage, and many sleepless nights with your new son."

They clinked glasses.

Hodgins thought back to the day over three weeks earlier when Councilman Smith was found in his long johns. "And I have an idea for a nanny. You'll love her."

Reviews are Golden

I would love to hear from you! Please consider leaving a review on your favourite social media platform, Amazon, or Goodreads.

Reviews mean the world to authors. Not only do we enjoy reading how you felt about the book, but they help other readers get a feel for a book in advance, and aid authors in marketing.

If you wish to hear about the progress of any of my books, please join my newsletter at: https://landing.mailerlite.com/webforms/landing/u0q5f2

Previous books can be found on Amazon at https://www.amazon.com/stores/Nanci-M-Pattenden/author/B01L5L2TSS

Thank you for coming on this adventure with me.

ABOUT THE AUTHOR

Nanci M. Pattenden is a genealogist and an emerging fiction writer, currently working on a collection of detective stories set in Victorian Toronto and an Urban Fantasy trilogy, Generation Witch. She also co-authors a funny paranormal series, D.E.M.ON. Tales.

She has completed the Creative Writing program at both the University of Calgary and the University of Toronto.

Nanci currently resides in Newmarket with her fluffy cat Snowball.

nanci@nancipattenden.com
www.murderdoespayink.ca
www.nancipattenden.com
@npattenden